Covenant
of Lies
The Healing Truth!

By Holly Spence

Monarch Publications, LLC books may be purchased
in bulk for educational, business, fundraising or sales
promotional use. For more information, please email
monarchpublicationsllc@yahoo.com

Spence, Holly 2010
Covenant of Lies the Healing Truth v2/ By Holly
Spence

ISBN 978-0-578-07683-6

Front and back cover designed by Timothy Hawkins
Back cover photo by Taylor Made Memories, LLC

This has been an amazing journey through the literary world. I have learned and discovered so much! In these times, the most awesome discovery has been the wealth and depth of African American and Christian Authors alike that are unknown but deserve to have just as much shelf time as a James Patterson or Danielle Steel.

Holly Spence

Table of Contents

About the Author

With a passion to know, learn and live God's Word, My wife has been anointed by God to deliver His Word to His people.

A native of Cincinnati, Ohio, Holly Spence is a graduate of the School of Creative and Performing Arts where she majored in Drama, Technical Theater Management and Vocal Music. She attended the University of Cincinnati, majoring in Chemical Technology. She currently serves as an OU Americas Sales LVC Program Manager for Oracle Corporation.

She is an author and playwright *("Servant Leadership: The Heart That Serves" & "Power of 10: Gaining Empowerment in 10 minutes, 10 words, 10 people", "STOP! You're Killing(is this You are or Your?)", "Covenant of Lies: the Untold Truth" and "Covenant of Lies: the Revealed Truth*), Conference Speaker and Workshop Facilitator. She is nominated as 2010 Female Author of the Year for the AAMBC Awards of San Antonio, Texas and Monarch Publications, LLC her publishing company, as Publisher of the year.

My wife has a true servant's heart. She is committed to covenant relationships and has a passion for God's Word. She is a covenant member of Overflow Ministries Covenant Church, where she submits and serves under the Godly government of Apostle Bennie and Pastor Delores Fluellen. She's an anointed psalmist, entrepreneur, and businesswoman. She's the mother of 3 beautiful children: Heather, Jehoshua and Joshijah-rapha. She's my best friend and covenant partner.

Vinnie C. Spence

Acknowledgements

Covenant Lies The Healing Truth is the last sequel in the Covenant of Lies trilogy.

To my editor and critic my Hermana: Melissa Allen some have come and gone, but you have stayed from the beginning. Thank you for the hours of edits.

Timothy Hawkins for 757 Media: I am so proud of you. I appreciate all that you have done and do. Check your email!

Dad and Mom (Apostle Bennie and Pastor Delores Fluellen) thanks for all that you do and your continuous support through my book projects.

To author Rebecca Campbell-Greene ("Sisters In The Name of Love" and "Diary" Series), Thank you for your reviews and feedback on the series. I am grateful for our divine connection.

Mrs. Anita M. Boclair, Founder of B.R.A.N.C.H.E.S Bookclub, my friend, family and agent: words cannot express my appreciation for you. Your vision and willingness to *"make it happen"* is just what every author needs.

Momma, thanks for reading "all" of the books. Your support and love is appreciated. I know it isn't always easy, but God knew best and He is getting the glory!

To my cousin Tracy J. Carter-Morgan, words are not enough to express my appreciation for your editorial skills. Now, you are in the book twice. I will let Pastor know you have a song on your heart.

To my sister Joy, who named the "Covenant of Lies" Series. Thank you. Well, your name is in the book twice.

My children Heather, Jehoshua and Joshijah-rapha remember in all that you do, make sure God gets the glory. Please Him and not man. I am proud of you and YOUR books look great!

To the stars in my sky and the honey in my tea, Mr. Vinnie Spence: I am grateful for your love and constant support. You weather it all, Monarch Publications, Monarch Divas, Monarch Jewels and Mary E. Thanks for being my Monarch.

__Chapter One__

Gilmore Park filled with the laughter and screams of children playing in the park's newly renovated playground area. Mothers are sipping on afternoon smoothies and baby strollers are rolling against the pavement. Joggers listening to their favorite musical selections with the wires from their headsets are flopping as they run. The smell of hotdogs and onions saturate the air from the local cart vendor. Pigeons are flying and landing near the legendary Ellis Family fountain. Local retirees and visitors of the park are feeding the pigeons and watching the ducks on the pond.

Beverly Martinez sits on the bench-watching children play, texting and checking email. Beverly is once a very high powered, well-known attorney in the city. After Carl Richardson broke off the affair with Beverly, she left Richardson and Associates devastated and distraught. Prior to leaving, her infamous pit bull attitude went on the attack defense ensuring that she would not walk away empty handed. Carl and his advisors thought it would be best to offer Beverly a severance package. That package did not set Richardson and Associates back much, but it is significant enough for Beverly to explore any opportunity she wanted, for at least the next five years without changing her current lavish life style.

The once vibrant, intellectual Yale graduate sunk into a deep depression in the weeks to follow her departure and separation from Carl. Beverly for a few days just would not let go and constantly called Carl's cell phone, to the point he changed his number. Beverly is smart enough not to harass him at the office or at home, especially after receiving a restraining order and letter explaining Carl's steps of legal threats.

Beverly stayed in her downtown, 4,400 square foot loft alone and did not leave for three months, ultimately feeding on the last of her canned goods. P her mortgage and other bills online.

After three months of crying and shredding everything that reminded her of Carl, Beverly packed her bags and left her loft. Beverly has not seen or heard of for over five years until Carl spots her a couple of weeks ago at Engine 13 restaurant one Sunday afternoon.

Beverly is a very attractive woman and heads turn no matter where she is or what she wears. Beverly is always dressed her best. Men taking their families for an afternoon stroll and older men alike appear captured by Beverly's beauty, as her leg crosses the other in a burgundy pencil skirt, with an Anne Taylor crème cashmere twin set. Her outfit complimented with a pair of patent Jimmy Choo pumps, a Marc Jacobs handbag and her neck draped with a timeless strand of pearls.

Beverly sits glimpsing at her watch, as the afternoon seems to pass away so quickly. Just as she makes a call on her cell phone, a man comes up from behind the bench and sits next to Beverly,

"Hey Beverly, here is the envelope…" Beverly looks up and takes the 8 ½ x 11 envelope.
"Hello Caleb, thanks for keeping this safe for me".

Caleb is a paralegal at Richardson and Associates and is smitten with Beverly, as most of the men are in the office. With the obvious crush, Beverly used it to her advantage to get work completed and any other dirt she wanted from Caleb.

"Beverly, I kept the envelope just like to you asks, I never looked in it and I never told anyone you gave me anything," says Caleb.
Beverly saw that the envelope still sealed with her original packing tape and initials.

"Good work Caleb, I can always count on you…"
Beverly stood up, grabbed her purse and the delivered
package, walked behind Caleb and stood over his
head and says "…you are such a jewel."

Beverly then kissed him on top of his head. You
would have thought that she planted a kiss in center of
his face the way he blushed and appeared as if he is
melting in his place. Caleb replies,

"Hey, thanks! You are a beautiful jewel yourself and
you know I would …" as Caleb talks he turns around
to discover that Beverly is gone and is nowhere in
sight, as if she had disappeared into thin air.

Caleb called out, "Beverly…Beverly…well easy
come, easy go…"

Chapter Two

Rose Farland Wellness Center is a beautiful facility situated on twenty-five lush acres of land. The drive into the facility is just as stunning as the tour around the grounds. Perennials for each season line the drive of the estate. Two ponds are home to Japanese Koi and water for local wild life. The east and west gardens have been designed for the most discriminating taste. Most of the residents, regardless of their current state, appear to enjoy the gardens and have often reminders that the flowers should not be picked.

Jessica is sitting by the window staring into the west garden. One of Jessica's doctors stops by; reviews her chart, attempts again to have dialogue with Jessica, and again met with silence. Jessica has been silent for weeks only having Stephanie and her team of doctors as visitors. Carl's appearances are just that, appearances. He has only stayed long enough to touch her hand or rub her hair. That is the most interaction Carl and Jessica Richardson the past weeks have had.

Joan, Jessica's second psychologist in the team comes in. "Mrs. Richardson what about getting some fresh air today? It's such a beautiful day outside."

Joan is attending to Jessica since her arrival. The wellness center's excellence in staffing is award winning. There is a five to one ratio for each team of doctors, nurses and orderlies, which is unheard of in most facilities. However, this standard of care with the daily patient cost comes with expectations. This facility receives recognition nationally to cater to those with financial stability. Celebrities as well as children of multi-billionaires are on the grounds of Rose Farland.

Joan helps Jessica to her feet. Joan ensures that she walks with Jessica several times a day to make certain the use of her legs is not lost due to her state of mind. As Joan walks with Jessica, she tries to talk to her in hopes that today, will be the breakthrough, she so desperately needs. Joan and Jessica reach the west garden with only a one-sided verbal exchange from Joan.

Jessica sits down on one of the many Italian marble benches that are located throughout the gardens. Joan continues to engage with Jessica by talking very generally about the weather and the beauty of the garden.

Joan's therapy with Jessica is interrupts as she runs to aid a nurse whose patient is running and screaming from the building and jumps in the pond. This causes great commotion among the other patients, with the exception of Jessica, who sits on the bench as if she is unaware of what is happening around her. Another young woman sits next to Jessica.

"Isn't this something, the number of crazy people around us? Clearly, that man needs a little more help, jumping in the pond like that. He needs a more permanent solution and Rose Farland is not it!" declares the young girl.

"Hello my name is...well, you probably don't even care, but I can tell, you really shouldn't be here. I think that you are grieving by a decision you have made, and now you do not know how to cope with it. Well...pick your chin up, Mrs. Richardson. There is someone that is going to need you."

The young woman got up and walked away. Jessica immediately turns to see who this young woman could be. The young woman turns back and waves. Jessica's heart leaped on the inside, the young woman reminded her so much of Jill. She smiles and returns the wave.

Chapter Three

Calvin Taylor's right arm is handcuffed to the bed
awakens and in a groggy voice says,

"What in the world? Where am I?"

"Sir, you are at Mercy North". The nurse pushes the
call button, "Yes, Mr. Taylor is now awake," says the
nurse.

With a look of confusion, Calvin says,

"Mercy North, what happened to me?"

The nurse replies, "Mr. Taylor you were in a terrible,
terrible accident on highway A-8..."

The doctor enters the room with the state trooper and detective with her. "Mr. Taylor, how are you feeling?"

"Mr. Taylor... who is Mr. Taylor?" Calvin responded. The state trooper chimes in, "Do you mean to tell me, he has lost his memory?"

The doctor continues, "I am Doctor Leanna Patel. Nurse Miller is explaining you were in a terrible accident on highway A-8 with severe head trauma and loss of blood. We had to do emergency surgery and were able to stop the internal bleeding. Is there anything that you remember about your accident a week ago?"

Startled, Calvin says, "A week... I have been unconscious a week?" Dr. Patel replies, "Yes, Mr. Taylor, I am afraid you have been in a coma for a week. We weren't sure if we were going to lose you."

"Oh my God…why am handcuffed to the bed?" says Calvin. Dr. Patel replies, "Uhmm, I will let…"

Jim Torrid steps right in, "Mr. Taylor, I am Detective Jim Torrid. State Trooper, Ken Mitchell found your car off A-8…." Nurse Mitchell and Dr. Patel left the room. "…When he called the tags in on your vehicle, he learned that it is registered to a Calvin Taylor. We have since been able to positively identify you as Calvin Taylor, who is wanted in questioning of a rape."

"RAPE! Rape of who, when? I do not know who I am and I wake up to you accusing me of rape? I want a lawyer and I want one now! Call those people at Richardson and Associates and tell them I want a lawyer!"

Detective Jim looks over at State Trooper Ken. Both looked perplexed as to why he is shouting out a legal firm, but has no idea of who he is; they were having their doubts.

Detective Jim continues, "Mr. Taylor, who should we ask for at Richardson and Associates? Do you know someone there?"

Calvin, with much further confusion and frustration and even louder voice shouted, "I HAVE NO IDEA, JUST CALL THEM. I DO NOT KNOW ANYONE THERE IT'S THE FIRST THING THAT CAME TO MY MIND…"

Dr. Patel and Nurse Mitchell rushed back into the room having heard Calvin's booming voice down the hall. "Mr. Taylor, please try to calm down…,"says Dr. Patel.

"CALM DOWN, CALM DOWN…I WAKE UP… NO MEMORY, IN PAIN, HANDCUFFED TO A BED AND ACCUSED OF RAPE…AND YOU WANT ME TO CALM DOWN…THIS IS RIDUCULOUS!" Calvin continues his rant while Dr. Patel instructed Nurse Mitchell to procure a sedative for Mr. Taylor. When she comes back into the room, she moves quickly to Mr. Taylor's IV and injects the sedative.

Dr. Patel continues to try to get Calvin to calm down. "Mr. Taylor, please calm down. This is not good for your blood pressure or the stitches on your wound. Please Mr. Taylor, calm down." With his armed cuffed to the bed, Calvin continues to jerk his arm attempting to break loose. Calvin is a very big man and proved to be intimidating, even to the detective and state trooper, who were both holding their hands on their weapons.

Calvin shouted, "LET ME OUT OF HERE, WHAT ARE YOU... WHAT IS SHE GIVING ME?"

Dr. Patel replies, "Mr. Taylor it's something to help you calm down." Almost instantly, Calvin became subdued. Everyone in the room is relieved.

The State Trooper began to ask questions and Dr. Patel asks that they continue to discuss Mr. Taylor outside his room, because subconsciously he could still pick up what they were saying. State Trooper Ken Mitchell inquires, "Doctor, has he actually lost his memory? He had enough memory to ask for a lawyer."

Dr. Patel replies, "Mr. Taylor appears to be experiencing an acute case of amnesia. I have seen many such cases, where such a traumatic accident causes amnesia that does not allow a patient to remember their name, if they are married or current events. There are also incidents where they can remember current events and all that they have learned such as grammar, reading, mathematics, even where their place of residence is, but can't remember their family members, children, parents or wife."

Detective Jim says, "So we could be waiting for some time for him to regain his memory?" Dr. Patel replies, "If he ever remembers."

Chapter Four

Selma Taylor returns to her room at North General after an hour of physical therapy. Standing by her bedside is Mark Swindoll with the most beautiful two dozen red roses.

"Hello, Mrs. Selma Taylor, seeing you walk in that door is a vision of beauty," says Mark.

"Well thank you Mr. Swindoll, that's exactly what I needed after the hour of torture." They both smile at each other with a chuckle. Mark takes over the nurse's duty and helps Selma into her bed.

Selma asks, "Are those beautiful roses for me?"
"Beautiful roses for a beautiful woman," Mark replies.

Selma holds her head down as if she is embarrassed. She has not received such sincere compliments from a man since marrying Calvin. In her mind, Selma begins to think back, trying to identify the last time she is made to feel as special as she did in that moment. As she continues to ponder her private question, tears begin to fall from her eyes. Selma makes every attempt not to begin her uncontrolled waterfall, but her inability to pin point appreciation from her husband causes the tears to fall. Mark immediately attends to Selma with his handkerchief from his suit jacket.

"Oh Selma, don't cry it's all true… you are beautiful, despite your current set of circumstances." As Mark wipes her first set of tears with his handkerchief, she continues tears he wipes with his thumb as he holds the right side of Selma's face in his hand. Selma looks up at Mark with an expression that instantaneously interrupts by Marcie's entrance into the room.

Mark immediately turns toward the door to greet Marcie. "Hello Marcie," "Hello, Mr. Swindoll," replies Marcie.

"I am glad to see you are doing much better. Your mother tells me you are able to leave soon?" says Mark.

"Yes, actually, I am being discharged today. I will officially be a visitor here at North General, but you may have a week or so to continue to supply red roses to my mother," replies Marcie in a slightly sarcastic tone.

Mark gives a quick smile and says his goodbyes. Selma has a look of disappointment with Marcie as

Mark leaves the room. Selma in a stern voice says, "Marcie Taylor, I can't believe you... how rude."

"I am rude? I think it is rude for him to give a married woman roses, and red roses at that! Mother, I am not a child and I can clearly see what has been happening for quite some time now..."

Selma interrupts, "Marcie you have no idea what is going on! Don't you think for one minute that just because you are with child you have concurrently reached adulthood? You are still a child and I am your mother!"

Marcie too stunned to get angry. She felt as if an arctic wind has just blown and froze her in place. Marcie's tears finally give her the courage to break her silence.

"Excuse me? Are you kidding me? You talk as if I have been a rebellious teenager, let me remind you Mommy, I is raped, RAPED REPEATEDLY BY

YOUR HUSBAND...." screams Marcie, "...I didn't ask for this and didn't ask for it the last year and half. But, here I am, walking around trying not to lose my mind, pregnant with my brother or sister, dealing with emotions that I shouldn't be faced with, when I should be identifying what University I will be spending the next four years...that at this point seems to be faded memories and lost hope. Instead, I have to contend with my child molesting father and adulterous mother who both appear to have forgotten that I AM THE CHILD IN THIS SCREWED UP..."

Courtney walks in, "Hey everything okay here?" Marcie with much anger, "NO COURTNEY, NO IT'S NOT..." Marcie explosively leaves the room.

Selma, in tears calls out, "Marcie, Marcie honey I didn't mean..."

Courtney makes every attempt to console Selma. "Courtney, I am so sorry that you have to walk in on this, I feel like such a failure. I have failed my child. I

did not protect her, with all that I went through as a…
I never wanted this for her; I never wanted this for
her…" Selma is crying hysterically.

"Mrs. Taylor, let me get something to help you relax."
Courtney makes the call for a sedative.

Selma, in her hysterics makes every attempt to climb
out of her bed to go after Marcie.

"Mrs. Taylor, what are you doing? Please calm
down…" Selma appearing to be emotionally out of
control says, "Courtney, I have to stop her, I need to
help my baby…"

Mrs. Taylor, I will look for her please don't hurt
yourself." Selma's sedative arrives just in time.

Chapter Five

Marcie, consumed by her mother's implication that somehow her pregnancy is her own fault, did not want to rationalize why her mother could make such a statement. Marcie sits in the floor's waiting area with only her thoughts and tears accompanying her. Between her tears and her thoughts, Marcie begins to get angry, but at each level of her personal inferno, the blast of tears diminishes her anger to further disbelief and bewilderment.

With cautious and genuine concern, Courtney peeped her head in the doorway of the waiting area asks, "Hey Marcie, want to talk?"

Marcie surprisingly looks up at Courtney and replies, "This is just all too much…" Courtney saunters into the waiting room and takes a seat next to Marcie. Marcie continues, "….I can't believe my mother, she actually says to me, *"don't you think for one minute that because you are with child you have simultaneously reached adulthood. You are still a child, and I am your mother!"* Can you believe that?"

Courtney looking with much suspicion says, "Well, did you say something that prompted that response?"

Marcie look at Courtney with much disgust and replies, "Yes, I walked in the room her beau and extracurricular activity, Mr. Mark Swindoll. He has given her a bundle of roses…red roses at that. He asks me about leaving the hospital, and I told him I am leaving today, but he had a week or so to continue to shower my mother with red roses..." Marcie folded her arms as she finishes her self-righteous speech.

Courtney chuckles to herself and replies, "Marcie, don't you see how that wouldn't sit well with your mother? She is your mother...I am not justifying what she said...it is definitely not your fault, but I am sure she is embarrassed and disappointed in your response. She responded without... maybe... not necessarily thinking about what she is saying." Marcie looks at Courtney. Courtney continues, "....again I am not justifying anything that your mother says, but you should be respectful. Do you know that she is having an affair with Mr. Swindoll or are you speculating?"

"If she is not having an affair, I would hate to see what one does look like," says Marcie.

"Marcie, there has been so much that you and your mother have gone through in the past two weeks, have the two of you had the opportunity to talk? You have the year and a half of abuse and now the unexpected birth of a child, which is a product of that abuse. That is a lot for you to handle, imagine how your mother must feel. Parents want nothing less than the best for their children…I haven't spoken with your mother, but I am sure that the series of events and your current situation is not her "best" for you!" says Courtney.

Marcie, still with tears in her eyes says, "Courtney, I know she probably didn't mean it, but it hurts so much!" Courtney embraces Marcie and did her best to console her through her embrace. Courtney reaches over to the side table to get Marcie some tissue.

"Here Ms. Marcie, wipe your eyes…where is that strong girl I saw last week? You were encouraging me on how things were going to be okay…what is your line? …*God is still in charge*"

Marcie smiles and says, "Yep, that's my line Ms. Courtney…and you're right God *is* still in charge."

Chapter Six

Joan is utterly shocked as she watched the latter part of Jessica's interaction with another patient. Jessica has been in her care for the past week and she is very concerned with her lack of responsiveness. Jessica's lack of participation in-group and individual sessions is a concern to most of her staff. Joan is very happy that today she has a different entry for Jessica's chart.

Joan, with much excitement asks Jessica, "Who is your new friend, Mrs. Richardson?" Joan with no response says, "Well, she appears to have taken interest in you."

After complete silence for a week, Jessica finally mumbled, "She reminds me of my daughter."

Joan, completely shocked, but did not want to miss this opportunity, continues to try to engage Jessica in conversation. "How old is your daughter, Mrs. Richardson?"

"My Jill, she is….seventeen," says Jessica. Joan is not sure how much more interaction she is going to get out of Jessica, but she is willing to push the envelope.

"What school does she go to?" says Joan. Then, just as suddenly as the conversation started, it begins to unravel. Jessica broke down into tears. Joan pulled a personal sized package of tissue from her pocket and comforts Jessica.

"Mrs. Richardson, it's okay. I know you are going to make it through this. You are *not* your circumstance. Your situation does not have control over you. You can control how you respond to this set of events that has separated you from your precious Jill."

Jessica continues to astonish Joan by continuing in conversation and addressing her by name, "Well Joan, it *appears* my circumstance has controlled me!"

"No, Mrs. Richardson it doesn't. Look at it this way…You were in the sunshine and it started to rain…"

Jessica interrupts, "Yes, and I is walking without an umbrella and I am soaked"

Joan smiles and continues "…yes that's right, but you haven't gotten this far in life without a little rain, and I am sure a woman of your caliber has had her share of storms."

Through her sniffles Jessica quietly responds, "Yes Joan, I have, but *this* storm has been brewing for a long time and I didn't take the necessary steps..."

Joan interrupts, "Okay... well, you shouldn't rehearse the negative, but you can acknowledge there is a storm."

Joan gave Jessica another tissue, as Jessica wipes her eyes, she says, "Oh I acknowledge there is a storm and..."

Joan interrupts, "...now you just have to remember how to dance in the rain." Jessica has not only talked for the first time in weeks, she also smiles. Joan is elated with her accomplishment.

.

Chapter Seven

Marcie and Courtney are still in the waiting room when they hear this loud squeal coming from the hallway. It is a man singing Natalie Cole's, "I Got Love on My Mind". Courtney and Marcie both look at each other in strange disbelief of the far from melodic sound filling the halls of North General. The bizarre sound immediately took Marcie away from her current disappointment with her mother.

Marcie could not resist, she ran to the door to see who is sounding like a wolf howling at an empty sky. Marcie is not able to see anyone as she peeks out the

31

door, but all she hears is *"I got love on my mind, I got love on my mind..."*

Courtney whispers, "Marcie who is it?" Marcie starts giggling, "I have no idea, I can't see him..."

"Well go out there," says Courtney. *"...and there's nothing particularly wrong, it's a feeling I feel inside, when I woke up early this morning, it is staring me straight in my eyes..."* Marcie turns and looks at Courtney. They both laugh. Courtney is urging Marcie to go out and see whom it is; just then, Marcie lets out a burst of laughter. She has the howler in her sight, "Sing now!"

Courtney stares at Marcie and mouths, "Who is it?" Marcie says, "He has love on his mind!" as she continues to laugh. As Marcie returns to her seat next to Courtney, John steps in front of the door.

"Marcie, are you laughing at me?" Courtney has the biggest look of surprise. John is not sure if she is surprised or horrified. "John that is you?" says Courtney. Marcie, doubles over in laughter, begins to mock John.

"Yeah, that is him and he has *love on his mind!*" Courtney tries not to laugh in front of John, but it is clear by the shaking of her shoulders and covering of her mouth that she is not doing a good job of holding everything in. John just stands there with his hands folded and starts laughing to ease the tension.

"John, whose love do you have on your mind?" says Marcie.

"Wouldn't *you* like to know, young lady?" says John.

Marcie gets up to leave the room, "Well, I don't have to ask Pat for a vowel or another spin, because I can solve this puzzle!" Marcie leaves the waiting room patting John on his shoulder. As she passes him, she turns to wink at Courtney. Courtney continues her inward chuckle. John steps into the waiting room and sits next to Courtney.

In a very serious voice and all kidding aside, John asks Courtney, "So, Courtney do you need to ask Pat for a vowel, or can you solve the puzzle too?" Courtney looks up at John and in complete shock. She did not want to assume, but she remains modest. "I think that I will need two vowels and a consonant."

John throwing caution to the wind says, "Well, Ms. Courtney Lewinsky, let me help you out, will you go out to dinner with me Thursday evening?"

Courtney smiles and says, "Oh John, that is sweet, but I have to work Thursday evening." John shook his head, "No you don't!" Courtney looks perplexed, "Oh, yes I do. I do the schedule…"

John interrupts her, "Yes, you do, but you are off this Thursday, and it would be my pleasure if you would accompany me to Le Grande Maison. Our reservations are at 7:00 p.m."

Courtney is completely shocked and very impressed by John's selection of restaurants, is further smitten when John kisses her hand and says, "J'ai hâte d'avoir une belle nuit avec vous, mademoiselle." Courtney just stares at John and he returns the favor. After what seems to be the longest minute ever, John says, "Oui?" Courtney knows exactly what he is saying now, and cannot help but say, "Oui!" John so much wants to express himself even further by fixing the most luxuriant kiss upon Courtney's lips, but he decides that moving too fast may not be the best move. Not to mention the call she receives to report to Emergency.

Chapter Eight

With the crisp breeze blowing and the warmth of the day's sun, Carl is still on his knees sobbing like a little boy. Henry falls down on Carl and wraps his arms around him. Carl and Henry rock back and forth both wailing in tears. Stephanie grabs Shane and Jill closer, preparing them for the worst.

Henry, hugging Carl keeps continually saying, "Carl, I am so sorry man, I am sorry man…" Shane continues to hold Jill's hand; Shane feels a greater intensity from Jill as she shakes from head to toe. Everyone is shedding their tears, still unaware of the outcome of the DNA results; a much public display of emotion from two former Miami U linebackers overshadows the results of the test.

Henry continues his repetitive apology with an additive plea to Carl, "…I am so sorry man, I am sorry, please forgive me, forgive me, forgive me, forgive me…"

Carl finally replies to Henry, "Henry, man I forgive you brother, I forgive you!" Carl and Henry fell to the ground rolling in their Armani suits. Shane comforts Stephanie, because her dam of strength breaches when she witnesses such forgiveness between her husband and long time friend.

Jill sits frozen, unsure of what this recent display of emotions from her Dad and Uncle Henry means. Shane consoling both his mother and Jill pierced the silence, "Please tell us the results Dad… please." Carl and Henry broke their rolling embrace, Henry says, "Carl…" Lying on his back, Carl wipes his eyes and sits up, looking at Jill and reads his letter. "Mr. Carl Richardson concerning the paternity of Jill Richardson you are 99.99% likely to be the father…"

Shane shoots straight up in the air literally forgetting that he has his mother and Jill on either side. "YES! OH GOD YES!!! I KNEW IT…. I KNEW IT!!!" proclaims Shane.

Jill gasps as if her body is taking in air for the first time. She covers her mouth and tears of joy flow as she lunges out for her Dad. He meets her embrace, and holds her in his lap rocking back and forth. "No matter what I told you, you will always be my baby girl. We have the test to prove it."

Shane, still jumping around the cemetery, screaming *"Yes!"* finally bends over and breaks down into tears. His mother, comes behind him and rubs his back, he stands and embraces her. "I told you Mom."
"Yes son, you had faith enough for all of us."

Henry, still on the ground wipes his eyes and rises to hold his family. Henry, with his colossal and extensive arm length wraps his arms around Shane and Stephanie. Through the tears Henry can be heard,

"I am sorry you had to go through this. I apologize, please forgive me." Carl and Jill join in the group hug. Only sniffles and tears express the sentiments of the group.

Shane breaks the circle by moving through the middle and grabbing Jill behind her ears and planting the longest, passionate kiss either of them has experienced. The kiss is so long, the parents were a little uncomfortable, but only Carl replies, "Well, I will save my money. I *know* there will be a wedding now!"

<u>Chapter Nine</u>

Beverly kicks her pumps off into her room. She quickly scans her mail she received and lays it on the kitchen counter. Beverly pours herself a glass of Riesling. She sits on her burnt orange Italian leather sofa and grabs the remote to see what the television would yield this sunny afternoon. Her cell phone rings and she immediately turns on her charm and answers the phone with a sultry seductive "Hello…oh nothing enjoying a glass of wine…yes I am alone…" With laughter, Beverly slings her hair and pushes it behind her ear, "…well, you have been so busy lately…. it requires that I spend most of my time alone…oh sure, you have been promising me that since I arrived back in town…work can't be that …well, you just tell him I said, you have someone more important to attend to…oh I would like that, but if you can't handle him, I know you can't handle me…what? Oh really? What a shame…maybe I will send a little cheer…OK, call before you come. I will make sure that I have slipped into something more comfortable for your arrival….until later."

Beverly hangs up the phone and immediately goes for the envelope Caleb gave her earlier. She opens the envelope and reviews the contents. She hit the envelope up against the palm of her left hand and says, "Oh yes, I think this would be a perfect time to send some Beverly Martinez cheer!" She laughs, finishes her wine and takes a shower.

Chapter Ten

The shift nurse, who is there to take her vitals, awakens Selma. While she is able to sleep for the last hour, it did not remove the reality of pain she felt concerning her conversation with Marcie. Selma continues to answer the nurse's questions and exchange pleasantries. Just as the nurse is leaving, Marcie walks into the room.

The shift nurse introduces herself to Marcie and continues out the door.

"Hi, Marcie!" Marcie strolls into the room and raises her hand, "Hi Mommy." Selma immediately begins her apologies. Marcie does not appear to be very receptive to her mother's repentance.

Marcie shakes her head and says, "Mommy, I know I was a little short with Mr. Swindoll, but my behavior didn't warrant your comment. I have so much that I am dealing with, not to discount what you are going through, but all that I am dealing with concerning you and Dad…it's just too much…" Marcie begins to cry. "…ugggh, I am so tired of crying, but that is all that comes out when I think…." Marcie continues to cry as she runs to her mother's bed.

"Marcie, I am sorry. I did not mean to upset you. It is not appropriate for me to make the statement I did. I know you are not to blame. Honey, you have to know that I never….NEVER wanted this for you. I have experienced things in my life….well...that haven't been…"

Marcie looks up at her mother, perplexed by her statement and in wonder of what she is going to disclose. Before Selma is able to make her confession, there is a knock at the door. A little aggravated by the interruption, Selma replies, "Yes, come in…" Marcie is wiping her eyes.

"Mrs. Taylor, Mrs. Selma Taylor?"
"Yes," says Selma.
"Hello, I am detective Jim Torrid. Is it possible for me to speak with you for a moment?"

Selma, very unsure of the reason for the visit says, "Sure, what is this all about?"
"Well Mrs. Taylor, can we talk alone?"
Selma quickly replies, "This is my daughter, whatever you have to say, you can say in front of her."
"Oh…okay, we have been looking for you for the past week. I am here to see you regarding your husband, Calvin Taylor, when is the last time you saw Mr. Taylor?" asks Detective Torrid.

Marcie looks at her mom and grabs her hand as Selma replies. "It's been a week, what's wrong? What has happened?"

Detective Torrid a little concerned by her response, "Mrs. Taylor, you haven't seen your husband in a week? Are you currently residing together?"

Selma very anxious replies, "Yes, please Mr. Torrid, what has happened to Calvin?"
"Mrs. Taylor, Calvin has been in a terrible accident…"
Marcie and Selma both gasp. "…his car is found on the side of the road off highway A-8 smashed into a tree. The car…totaled. Mr. Taylor required emergency surgery to stop internal bleeding…"

Selma and Marcie both interjecting their comments of disbelief, Marcie finally asks, "Is he dead?"
"Detective Torrid, just tell us, did Calvin die in the accident?" says Selma.

Detective Torrid continues, "No, he is not dead, but…"

"But what?" says Selma,

"….he just woke up from a week long coma and has lost his memory."

"What? How much of his memory has been lost? Does he know who he is?" says Selma.

Detective Torrid looks for a chair and asks, "May I sit down?"

"Oh, please yes…yes, sorry about that," says Selma. "No problem, I know this comes as quite a shock. I hate to have to deliver this to you while you are in the hospital, but I am hoping that maybe you can shed some more light on the situation. You mentioned that you have not seen him in a week. The last time you saw Mr. Taylor, is that before or after you arrived in the hospital?" Selma hesitates to answer. She is working up the courage to respond, while being comforted by Marcie holding her hand.

"Mr. Torrid, Calvin is the reason I am in the hospital!"
says Selma with her head held high. Marcie in that
split second is proud, as well as surprised by her
mother's sudden display of bravery.

Detective Torrid looks up immediately from his pad
of paper at Selma's response. "Mrs. Taylor, I am sorry
to hear that."
"Thank you," says Selma.
"Mrs. Taylor, I have more of a personal question for
you. I mentioned to you previously that Mr. Taylor is
wanted for questioning, in a rape case. Did Mr. Taylor
rape you?" As Selma continues to hold her head high,
Marcie felt as if she has frozen in place.

Chapter Eleven

Calvin, rubbing his head, wakes up and is startled to see a gentleman standing next to his bed.

"Excuse me, may I help you? Who are you?" says Calvin. The man just looks at him; Calvin reaches for his call button when the man finally broke his silence. "Hello Mr. Calvin Taylor…"

"Well, that's who they tell me I am. Are you from Richardson and Associates? I woke up today and learned there is an accusation against me. Man, I don't even know who I am."

"Mr. Taylor, why don't you start from the beginning, and I will take notes."

Calvin baffled says, "That is the beginning. I literally woke up earlier today with the Doctor introducing herself and asking me what I remembered about my accident a week ago. I did not know that I was in an accident, and then she told me I had emergency surgery to stop internal bleeding. To make matters worse, a Detective Torrid introduces himself and tells me that I am wanted for questioning in a rape. I immediately asked for a lawyer."

"Well, Mr. Taylor you did the right thing. You have no memory at all? Do you have any memory of your family? Your wife and daughter?"
Calvin totally dismayed. "What? I have a wife and daughter? Just one daughter? Maybe if I see them, it will help me remember. Do they know that I am in the hospital? Oh, this is too much, I wouldn't want them to see me…I can't even remember who they are..."
Calvin breaks down in tears.

Dr. Patel walks through the door, as the gentleman is preparing to leave. "Mr. Taylor, I will visit you tomorrow, and I will let you get some rest." Before Calvin could get himself together, the man is shaking Dr. Patel's hand and heads out the door.

"You don't have to go," says Calvin.

Dr. Patel replies, "Oh excuse me, I didn't know you had a visitor."

"Yes, he is from Richardson and Associates. Thanks for calling them for me Dr. Patel.

Dr. Patel runs to the door, but the man is gone. She turns back to Calvin and says,

"Mr. Taylor I didn't call Richardson and Associates. I have the number here for you to call. What did that man say his name is?"

Calvin, concerned and confused says, "When I woke up he is standing over my bed. He never did say his name, now that I think about it."

Dr. Patel immediately pulls Detective Torrid's card out of her pocket. "Mr. Taylor, I am going to call the police. Detective Torrid has to know about this incident.

Dr. Patel calls Detective Torrid only to get his voicemail. "Mr. Taylor, I left a message. I also suggest that you call Richardson and Associates immediately."

Calvin, still in tears says, "Dr. Patel, who am I? I am even more concerned with what kind of man I am. That man mentioned that I have a wife and a daughter. If I have been in a coma for a week and no one has been looking for me…what does that say about this so called Calvin Taylor, the man?"

Chapter Twelve

Shane finally lets his grip loose on Jill and rests his
head Jill's forehead. Shane whispers to Jill, "I love
you." Jill replies a little embarrassed by Shane's kiss,
"And I love you Shane McFinley, but do you realize
you just kissed me in front of our parents?" Shane
smiled, "Are you a little embarrassed?"
"Yes," says Jill.
"Well, I bet not as embarrassed as they are?" Jill
could not help but laugh, Shane always knows how to
get her to laugh.

Shane breaks with Jill and announces "Well do you think celebration is in order over a nice meal at…..oh, Engine 13?"

Stephanie just shook her head, "That's my son; always ready for a meal?" Carl and Henry were standing next to each other hugged up still wiping tears. Stephanie, sensing that the atmosphere is still emotionally charged, suggested to Shane, "maybe Uncle Carl would like to spend some time with Jill alone."

Everyone looks to Carl for a response, Jill replies, "Daddy, we should go see Mom and let her know the good news?"
Carl, trying to get himself together looks to Stephanie and says, "Do you think that would be a good idea?"
Stephanie smiles, "I think that would be a great idea. Good news is exactly what Jessica needs right now. I would - of course, discuss it with her doctor prior to making the announcement. Jessica needs you more than ever now."

Jill hugs her father "Daddy, let's go tell Mom."
Henry, giving Carl a pat of reassurance on the back
says, "Man, let's get our families back in order." Carl
and Henry embrace again. Everyone says their
goodbyes, while Carl and Jill walked toward the car.
Henry, Stephanie and Shane walk a little behind in an
unusual silence for such a joyous occasion. Stephanie
hugs Henry around his waist and Henry returns the
favor.

Henry and Stephanie walk in each other's arms in
silence. She is waiting for the right moment to speak.
She wants to see how Henry is really doing, but there
is actually something in her that is enjoying the
silence. Stephanie felt a sense of relief and a stranger
feeling of wanting to be alone. Since this shocking
news, Stephanie has been the supportive glue that
holds her family together. She is constantly reassuring
Henry that they can make it through this trial, but she
is now wondering if she believed those very words
she'd spoke not so long ago.

Shane is unable to harness his excitement, and is doing flips in between the stones in the cemetery. Stephanie, not completely shocked by Shane's shenanigans, instantaneously recalls his elementary schools years. She teases, "Shane McFinley..." as she releases a little chuckle, "...if you don't harness that energy!" Shane walks back to his mom, grabs her and picks her up.

"I am so happy Momma!" boasts Shane as he swings Stephanie around in circles. Stephanie very discreetly urges Shane to put her down. Shane continues with his acts of folly, joyfully playing with his mother and expressing his delight of being right about Jill not being his sister. During this brief playful encounter, neither Shane nor Stephanie noticed that Henry is not walking with them.

Stephanie says, "Shane where is your father?" Just then, Shane spins his mother around and she gets a glimpse of Henry.

Stephanie yells out "Henry!? Henry!?" Shane put his mother down and turns to see why she is releasing such an alarming shout. Henry is doubled over and slowly falling to the ground.

Chapter Thirteen

Since leaving the cemetery, Jill is incessantly
expressing her joy that the ordeal concerning her and
Shane is done. Carl agrees with baby girl with a
simple "Yep!" when he thinks he can get a word in.
Jill normally is not so talkative, but Carl did not blame
her for her excitement. While this should be a blissful
occurrence, Carl still has mixed feelings concerning
Jessica and her years of deceit. *"But how can I
consider leaving her, when she forgave me?"* Carl did
not expect this, not after all these years. Maybe he just
needs one good cry with Jessica, as he has
experienced with Henry. He is not sure, but there is
definitely part of him that just does not want to deal
with it right now.

Carl pulls into Rose Farland Wellness Center where the guard who immediately greets and welcomes the Richardsons past the gate. Although Carl has not visited with Jessica regularly, the expectations are that the guard knows every family member of patients within the Rose Farland Center. This type of customer service, Rose Farland is famous.

Jill, still in her joyous state squeals with excitement, "Daddy! I cannot wait to tell Mom, this will be great news! How do you think she will react? Relieved? I am sure she will be excited as..."

Carl interrupts, "Baby girl, don't forget Aunt Stephanie suggests that we speak with her doctors prior to mentioning anything to her."

"I know Daddy, but I can't imagine..."
Carl interrupts Jill again, "Jill, I know you are excited...but I don't want you to be disappointed if the doctor recommends that we not tell your Mom.

She is having a very difficult time and at last report....well..."

"Daddy? What...what has happened?" interjects Jill.

"...I hesitate to tell you, and have not shared with you the reports from the doctors trying not to overwhelm you or cause you any unnecessary worry, but your mother hasn't spoken a word since she arrived and that is a great concern."

Jill, with a slight plead says, "Daddy, you have to stop treating me like I am a baby...I am growing up, you know..." they both exchange a smile, "...this situation alone has definitely moved me up on the *"growing up meter"*, even you would have to agree with me there Daddy..." Jill gives her "baby girl" grin, hoping to lighten the mood some with her father and to make him feel comfortable.

Carl could not help but agree, "Yes it did but as your father, I just..."

Carl starts to get choked-up. Jill grabs her Dad's hand. "...I hate that it had to be such a potentially devastating circumstance that moved you up that meter. I just hope you understand, as your father, I did not, and still to this day do not take for-granted my responsibility that is bestowed on me from God. It is my privilege and heart's desire to care for provide and protect you, and I feel as…as…" Carl is continuing to get choked-up fighting extremely hard not to let Jill see him break down.

Jill very gently squeezes her Dad's hand and says, "Daddy, although this hasn't been the easiest thing to deal with, and quite frankly, I would have preferred that this situation wouldn't have been the mercury for my "growing up meter", but it is; and I am trusting God to bring us out with peace. As Pastor always says, *"Nothing missing, and nothing broken."* That has been my prayer for us all Daddy. I cannot imagine what you are going through and how this makes you feel. I will admit that I am concerned about you and Uncle Henry's relationship, and if things will ever be the same. I am even more, well…worried would be the better word, concerning you and Mom. I have to give that worry over to God daily or it would consume me. Daddy you can rest assured that you have not failed me in any way throughout my life, you have always been there, and I am learning daily that you are a true reflection of God in the earth as my Daddy, and I love you for it."

Carl could not hold back the tears any longer. His wall of strength crumbles and his courtyards of vulnerability are exposed. Carl and Jill fall into each other's arms. Jill could not help but break down in tears after seeing her father's tears. This day is full and charged emotionally. Carl pulls a handkerchief out and begins to wipe Jill's face. Carl is getting much pleasure in Jill allowing him to take care of her, even in this small manner. Carl sniffs and says, "Well, this may be one of the last times I get to do the little things for my baby girl…"

Jill grins, "Daddy you still have time…I am not getting married tomorrow!" They both laugh when Carl's cell phone rings.

Carl looks at his phone, "Let me grab this really quick, it's the office." Jill nods in agreement. Jill looks out of the car window admiring the meticulous grounds of Rose Farland when her father's voice identifies as one of shock and disbelief. "What? Are you sure? Well…yeah, if it is who I think. I will not be able to handle this today. Sure, send someone over to do the interview. "Okay, keep me posted." Carl hung up the phone wondering if the drama would ever cease. Jill immediately asks, "Daddy, everything ok?" Carl, still very perplexed replies, "Just some unusual events in the office. You go on in; I need to make another call just to check on something." Jill gladly accommodates her father's request and they agree to meet in the lobby. Jill even agrees to have her Mom's doctors paged to speed things up.

When Jill leaves the car and is at a safe distance, Carl lays his head down on the steering wheel. "God, this can't all be happening?" Carl cries aloud. Carl works hard to get it all together so he can go in with Jill to see his wife. Carl is feeling very unsure of himself and has to admit that he has not felt this way since being a boy, wet behind the ears, during his college days. Carl is seeing flashes of Jessica and is feeling as if he is so out of sorts he did not know if he could actually see her.

Carl shaking his head at himself says, "Buck up Carl Richardson and get a hold of yourself man!" Carl wipes his eyes and proceeds to the entrance of the Wellness Center.

Chapter Fourteen

Carl jumps out of the car whispering a prayer for strength. He looks down at his suit, realizing his tailored Armani, covered with grass from the cemetery. A slight grin comes to Carl's face thinking about him and Henry rolling in the grass in the cemetery. Brushing his pant legs, he is not sure about seeing Jessica, but he is sure that he did not want to look as if he's been rolling around on the ground. Carl thought to himself *"What a day!"*

When Carl walks through the door of Rose Farland, Jessica's team of doctors are approaching Jill. "Perfect timing…let's go into consultation room #4." says Joan. Joan continues, "Mr. Richardson, I have some very good news. I just finished updating Mrs. Richardson's chart and updating the team. She spoke today. Not only did she speak, she held a conversation with me...We are very excited!"

Jill, already a bundle of excitement stood to her feet and let out a resounding "YES! Oops, I'm sorry, but that is such exciting news, and we have even more good news to share with my mom that we think will help with her recovery." Carl, elated to see Jill's bliss, responds with a lot less enthusiasm. Not intentionally, he is trying extremely hard to share in Jill's excitement, but he is still processing his own feelings. "My daughter is referring to the incident that brought her mom to this point. As I mentioned when I checked Jessica in, I had just learned that there is the possibility that Jill is not my daughter. We have since had DNA testing to confirm she indeed is my daughter...so..." Carl feels tears beginning to build; he is determined not to have another break down, not four in one day. "...so we wanted to make certain it is okay to share this news with her. You don't expect that this will make things worse, do you?"

The doctors all responding at the same time "Absolutely not, oh this is great news, yes it could speed her recovery."

Joan chimes back in, "Mr. Richardson, your wife needs every good and positive event shared with her to help with her recovery process. This may be the very thing that gets her back on track…oh this is…"

Carl interrupts, "Doctor, what triggered her to talk today?" Joan, with a smile on her face looks at Jill.

"I talked her into walking in the courtyard; there is a patient that decided to play in the fountain. While I am helping the staff member with that patient, Mrs. Richardson had a visit from another patient who reminded her of your lovely daughter…and now having met her, I understand that is enough to make anyone talk. Mr. Richardson, watch out sir, she could be a heart breaker."

Jill and Carl smiled at each other. "Doc, she has already stolen someone's heart, and he has no bones about telling the world."

__Chapter Fifteen__

6 Months Later

Marcie arrives home after a very long day. After school, she went out with Courtney to help her with some of the last of her wedding plans. She is so happy for Courtney and John. John is like a knight in shining armor for Courtney, at least in Marcie's eyes.

Seeing John and Courtney's blossoming relationship over the past six months gives Marcie some hope that she will heal, and find *"Mr. Right"*, who can love her, and not abuse her. Marcie and Courtney established a very strong bond during her hospital stay; Courtney shared her own life experience of rape and abuse. With counseling and Courtney's late night conversations, Marcie is walking all right on her road of healing and forgiving. Courtney could not exactly understand how Marcie is so willing to forgive her father so quickly, but she begins to come around when she gives her life back to Christ.

The house is dark. Marcie realizes her mother must have been pulling another late night. Marcie's mother is fortunate enough to get a teaching job at her high school and works as a server at night to help supplement her income and ensure ends met. Marcie wonders how many nights she is actually working. When she goes to the diner on evenings with Courtney and John, she expects to see her mother but she is not there. Marcie assumes she is out with Mark Swindoll. Marcie decides keeping the peace is more important than confronting her mother about Mr. Swindoll. After all, she deserves to be happy as well. Marcie is ready to attend counseling with her father, but her mother on the other hand is adamant about not being in the same room with *"that man"* as she calls him.

After two months of memory loss, Calvin Taylor gains most of his memory concerning his abusive behavior. When Marcie and Selma took the stand in Calvin's rape case, his regret and disbelief about his behavior is evident by the outburst of tears. The outbursts were so bad, that the judge would call for a recess. Marcie, feeling sorry for her father, finally convinces her mother to drop the charges, because he just did not know and seemed to be genuinely apologetic.

Selma finally agrees, but continues with the divorce proceedings. Calvin seems to be dragging his feet concerning that issue. He tells Selma he wants his family back, but Selma is not interested in hearing that at all. She finally breaks away from Calvin's controlling grip and she is not willing to take the risk.

Marcie slowly walks down the hallway to her bedroom, dreading each step on her swollen feet. Her mother recently hung her baby pictures; the apartment is slowly becoming more like home every day. It is definitely very different from the seven-bedroom mansion they lived in just months ago, but it is a happier space and has a feeling of security.

Marcie turns the knob on her bedroom door, walkes in and turns on the light. She gasps with fear when she sees her father sitting on her bed and he says, "I have been waiting for you."

Chapter Sixteen

Jessica is up, dressed and had breakfast, all before most of the patients at Rose Farland were even stirring, with the exception of Mrs. Rankin, whose worship music you can hear every morning. Mrs. Rankin's encouragement over the past month had really brought Jessica to a place of healing. Jessica often wonders how Mrs. Rankin is so encouraging to her, but unable to draw from her own well for herself.

Mrs. Rankin steps into Jessica's doorway, "Well sir, you look very special this morning! All ready to go home dearie?"

"Yes, Ma'am I am!" resounds Jessica. Jessica stands with her hands on her hips and her infamous smile plastered across her face.

"Well, I won't interrupt your progress, I will see you before you leave." says Mrs. Rankin as she walks away with such a stellar of grace. Jessica continues getting her things together. While she had spent some weekends at home over the past three months, being home permanently is something Jessica is unquestionably looking forward to being home. She also thinks that it would help her and Carl get back to the place of mending versus coexisting.

Over the past six months, Carl participated in all of the counseling sessions and visits every other day. Still, Jessica knows that Carl is hollow toward her. On the weekends, he is pleasant but removed. Carl is not touching Jessica. Jessica, knowing Carl's sexual appetite, wonders what he is doing to satisfy his desires. In an effort to stay focused, she tries to remove it out of her mind. Carl never says he forgives

Jessica during their counseling sessions. The only thing he says is *"I am working on it."*

Jill on the other hand, is full of mercy. Jessica's interactions with her are pure pleasure. Jessica knows that Jill is wrapped-up in her affection of Shane, that everything in her world is fine. Jessica did not question it, she welcomes the love she receives from Jill. She is happy to get it from someone, but the person she wants it from the most is Carl.

Last weekend before coming back to Rose Farland, Jessica brought the outfit she wants to wear home. She picks Carl's favorite St. John piece, then had her manicure, pedicure and hair done in the Rose Farland salon the day before. Today, the on-staff makeup artist is coming to help her with her make up before leaving. She wants to look her best when Carl picks her up. Jessica removes her cards from around her room; most of the cards were from Jill and Stephanie. She has more mail in the drawer that she has never opened. She assumes that most of the cards were probably from other church members, but she never opens any mail that came to Rose Farland, only mail that Jill or Carl brought in. Jessica thought that opening mail delivered to the Wellness Center somehow indicates that she lives here, which for the past six months honestly she has.

With all the personal amenities and luxurious suites, it certainly is not home. Jessica thinks about Carl holding her in his arms, brings her to tears. Jessica sits on the window seat looking out at the fountain and whispers a prayer, *"God, please reunite Carl and me. I have accepted your forgiveness and have forgiven myself. Soften his heart and allow him to be in tune to Your Spirit…to hear your voice. Father Your Word says…what you have joined together let no man put asunder…I declare Your Word over our marriage in Jesus' name."*

Jessica wipes her tears and empties her drawer of mail. She threw the mail in a very nice Rose Farland bag. Most of the mail is cards, and she has two 8 ½ x

11 envelopes with no return address. She does not remember when they came, but just threw them in the bag. Jessica is looking forward to moving on and not living in the past.

Chapter Seventeen

Henry is standing in his family room looking out the window into the back yard. The Miami sun is shining as usual, but Henry has one consuming thought, Stephanie. In between sips of coffee, Henry lets out a sigh that sounds so weary and he whispers *"Stephanie, I miss you...I miss you so much..."*

Henry's eyes begin to well up; he is past the point of trying to be strong and deny his emotions. As the tears fall he cries out to God, *"Father, bring her back to me, give me the words to express my undying love for her. Allow her trust to be restored in me, shine through me oh God, that she sees You and not the sins of my past. Rekindle that spark in her heart toward me*

giving me the opportunity to shower her with affections of safety and security. Grant me another chance Father in Jesus' name...Let it be so... Amen!
The phone rings; Henry quickly wipes his tears and runs toward the phone in hopes that it is Stephanie. Anxiously he answers, "Hello? Good morning Pastor, no...no...I am hanging in there, well I expected, hoped you were Stephanie. No, I have not heard from her. Yeah...yep... We are still on for this afternoon; ok I will see you then."

Pastor Matthews is a great support for Henry in past six months. He is hoping that Carl can join him in counseling, but he has yet to come. He could not exactly blame him, but their daily talk is reducing to conversations every couple of weeks. Henry is missing his support as well...but he is giving Carl the space he thinks he needs.

Shane comes down the stairs his jovial, love bitten self. "Morning Dad, what's up man?" Shane is definitely able to draw a smile on Henry's face. Shane is so supportive and forgiving; he is a constant positive source for Henry.

Shane begins to shadow box with his Dad, "Boy, you don't want none of this." Over the past six months, Shane has shot up reaching right under Henry who is six foot two. Shane grabs his dad by the legs and picks him up.
Shane proudly says, "Now what?"
Carl says, "Put me down, that's what!!" They both laugh and fell to the floor.

Henry looks at Shane and the tears start to fall, Shane grabs his dad and says, "It's going to be alright, and Daddy…Mom's coming back. She loves you and so do I."

Chapter Eighteen

Jessica's doorbell rings to her room. "Just one moment" calls out Jessica.

There stood the makeup artist and the concierge with a basket full of goodies. "Come in, what do we have here?"

"Mrs. Richardson, this is just delivered for you. It looks like everyone wants to help celebrate your last day here at Rose Farland. Best Wishes."

"Thank you!" says Jessica.

As the make-up artist is setting up, Jessica sits the huge basket on the table wondering who sent the basket. Her heart wants it to be from Carl, but she is slightly disappointed as she read the card, *"Sorry I*

couldn't make it today to see you off, best wishes.
Your friend - Beth"

Beth is a volunteer that visits patients on the wing providing encouragement or just companionship for the guests. Over time, it seems that Beth only came to see her, and their bond grew from there. Jessica shares Jill's senior picture and Beth would share pictures of her five-year-old son, ironically named Carl. As Jessica looks through the cellophane, she smiles. Her heart is so full of delight; but seeing Carl will culminate it all.

Chapter Nineteen

Marcie wakes up screaming, "NO!!! NO!!!!"

Jill runs out of the bathroom, "Are you ok?" Marcie stares at Jill, looking around the room trying to get her bearings.

Jill comes next to her bed, "Marcie are you okay?"

Marcie's mother comes through the door, "Marcie honey, are you ok?" Selma walks to the other side of the bed, sits down, and lays her hand on her growing stomach.

"Marcie, honey you okay?"

Marcie breathes a sigh of relief, "Yes, I am fine, it is another nightmare…."

Jill and Selma both relaxed and relief you can see in both of their eyes as they look at one another.

"…It is so real. I is coming home after a long day at school and helping Courtney with wedding plans. I walked into my bedroom turns on the light….and…Daddy is sitting on my bed and he says…"

Marcie breaks down crying. Jill holds her in her arms. Selma sits on the other side of the bed trying not to spill her venom of hatred for Calvin. Every nightmare Marcie is experiencing is like a dart to her heart. Oh how Selma wishes she had left this man sooner. She rubs Marcie, trying to sooth her nerves, knowing that each time she experiences this type of trauma the baby experiences it also. Selma wants Marcie to consider not keeping the baby very early on, but that is not an option for Marcie. Marcie is growing exactly how Selma intended: loving, God fearing and full of faith.

Chapter Twenty

Carl awakes to the announcement *"Welcome to Miami International Airport where the time is 10:24 a.m. On behalf of your Pensacola flight crew, it has been a pleasure serving you."*

Carl wipes his face. He has been traveling all morning. He knows he is cutting it close to time to pick up Jessica. Although his flight is not delayed, he has to rely on traffic not being a beast. He also has to pick up Jill from Marcie's house, but thank goodness, that is on the way. Marcie and Selma live closer to the city now.

Carl continues to rub his hands across his face. He could not help but think about what his life is going to be like with Jessica back in the house. He knows she is working so hard to get things back to the way they were. All his questions about when and how long the affair took place, Jessica willingly supplied. He also understood why she forgave him so easily because she is hiding her own indiscretion from years earlier. She disclosed that she is the one that wanted to keep the affair hidden and that Henry on several occasions wanted to tell the truth about the brief fling. With that information, Carl's heart toward Henry began to soften even more, even though their relationship is not back to normal either.

Over the past six months, weeks at a time go by before Carl would talk with Henry. He misses talking to Henry, and even in this case he knows that Henry would steer him back into Jessica's arms, even if he did not want to go. Part of Carl is satisfied with being unforgiving because he wants Jessica to hurt the way he is hurting.

Carl begins to shake his head to himself, *"God help me… this animosity in my heart for Jessica is not of you and I know it. Soften my heart…Allow me to desire her, want her, need her and love her …God I know she can never feel my hurt… so expecting her….Oh God, it's not about her it's about me…deal with me God, deal with my heart."*

The plane pulls up to the gate and the *"fasten seat belt"* light goes off. Carl moves to get in the aisle first to do a preliminary stretch of his legs and arms. When Carl turns on his cell phone, there are several missed calls, half of which were from Jill. Just as he is checking his phone messages, the phone rings again. Carl answers the phone.

"Good morning Baby Girl! Yes, I am on the way…did you and Marcie have a good time? Really, is she okay? Good… it is good you were there for her…yes, I am out and about… I will be there soon…ok…love you too!"

Since the trial, Jill and Marcie have reconnected. Carl sees much of Jessica's warm and helpful spirit within Jill. Marcie often expresses her appreciation for Jill, reconnecting with her and not causing her to feel like an outcast. Those young ladies have been through a lot over the past few months, but the children appeared to be bouncing back quicker than the adults are.

Carl picks up his phone to make another call while walking to the car. "Hey, it's me…I is just calling to let you know I made back in town, and well…I will talk to you soon….bye."

Carl dodges through the airport traffic to go to the garage where his car is. He arrives at his car, opens the trunk and drops in his Hartman duffle. As he is getting in the car, he notices an 8 ½ x 11 envelope under his windshield wiper. He looks around to see if he can see anyone watching him. Then, he takes the envelope and gets in the car.

Carl can smell a sweet, floral, familiar fragrance on the package. For one minute he thinks, "...*Naw it couldn't be...*" but he knows very well; and when Carl opens the envelope, which confirms his suspicions.

Chapter Twenty-one

After Henry's heart attack scare, Stephanie continues
to be supportive and nurses him back to health. They
are both cordial, but it is obvious the Jessica/Henry
scandal has taken its toll on Stephanie. Henry, in his
guilt-ridden state, notices Stephanie's fallen
countenance. He often tells Stephanie *"Don't leave
me, take whatever time you need, but don't leave. We
have too much invested."* Stephanie reassures Henry
each time that she has no intentions on leaving him,
but she has not properly processed her feelings. She
shares with Shane that she will be spending some time
at the beach property. He is so sweet and supportive
and actually encourages her to go and do whatever it

is going to take to mend her relationship with his father.

The morning after Henry's last doctor's appointment, Stephanie packs a few items, sits on the edge of the bed next to Henry, kisses him on his forehead and tells him, *"I need some time. Don't worry, I am not leaving you, just need some time."* Henry sits up in the bed and holds Stephanie. He does not want her to go, but he knows it is best to let her have her space. He kisses her cheek and then her ear. Stephanie pulls away with her head down and walks away. That is thirty days ago.

Meanwhile, Stephanie awakes to the waves and the smell of salt water. She sits on the deck of their beachfront property in Destin, Florida. It is such a peaceful place. She loves their retreat home. Although the house, holds so many memories, Stephanie feels it is exactly what she needs to clear her head and spend some much needed alone time, just her and God.

Stephanie often pauses in her morning reading just to admire the calming ocean and watch the Seagulls fly above the ocean's surface. She closes her eyes and just breathes in the morning air.

Stephanie texts Shane daily just to let him know she is okay. Shane calls every couple of days if she did not call. He calls himself "laying down the law", by telling his mother he is doing okay with the *"needing her space thing"*, but she has to check in. Stephanie without argument agrees and chuckles, she knows Shane is right.

Henry only sends three word texts of *"I love you!"* It is not until her third week away that she starts to reply *"I love you, too!"* Stephanie's cell phone ringing interrupts her peace. She looks down and chuckles to herself… *"Speak of the angel…* Hello Shane Richardson, how is Mommy's man?" Stephanie has said that to Shane since he was a little tot. He is definitely growing into a fine, God-fearing young man. He is one of which any mother can be proud.

"Oh Mom…." says Shane and then indulging his
mother says, "….Mommy's man is just fine…"
Stephanie could not help but allow her mouth to form
a blushing smile.

"…How's Mommy's man's Momma?"
Stephanie smiles and laughs again, "Momma is doing
well. Sitting on the deck, gazing at the ocean, feeling
the morning rays on my face and reading my
Word…How is your Dad? Is he eating right? Is he…"
Shane interrupts, "Mom he is doing all that…I am
sure he would do better if you came home, it's been
thirty days. When are you coming home?" There is an
uncomfortable silence.

"Son, I will definitely be there for graduation."
Shane, with a little disappointment says, "Mom…are
you…okay?…. it's okay, and do what you have to do,
because when you come back, I want it to be for
good." Stephanie did not make any promises to Shane,
she just changes the subject.

"How is Jill doing? You two remaining holy?" asks Stephanie, already knowing the answer to the question, or so she hopes.

"Momma, now you know, before I kept myself for you and dad...but now... I am doing it for me." Stephanie is beaming with pride, balls her hand in a fist, and motioned to herself *"YES!"* Shane wanting to be completely honest told his mother, "Now, I will tell you...sit down Mom, we have a close call, but we both backed it up and said hold on, hold on!" Stephanie rolled her eyes in her head, "Lord boy, you don't have to..." Shane interrupts and says, "Mom, I'm not telling you to make you uncomfortable, I am telling you to be accountable. I took a vow with you and Dad and I want you to know I am honoring my vow."

In that moment, Shane's wisdom pierced Stephanie's heart. She thinks about her vow she made to Henry, and that it is for better or worse. Stephanie says, "Yes, son you make me proud; and Jill is getting a jewel of a husband."

"Well Mom, you and Dad can take credit for that in spite of it all. Who I am, I learned from you both. Watching your marriage…this thing with Dad and Aunt Jess is early in your marriage. I do not know anything about that. I can only attest to what I have experienced since I have been around you and Dad. You have been the picture of a Godly marriage. That example is what I know and have seen that's what I take to my future with Jill."

The tears begin to fall down Stephanie's face. She knows this is God speaking to her through Shane and thinks, *"All is not lost."*

Chapter Twenty-two

Carl pulls up to Selma Taylor's apartment, jumps out and put the envelope in the trunk before Jill comes out of the house. Carl waves at Selma who is standing at the door. Jill comes out of the apartment in a slight jog.

"Good morning Daddy!"

"Good morning baby girl!" Carl takes Jill's bag and opens the door for her to get into the car.

Jill is just as talkative as she was the day she had learned Shane was not her brother. Carl knows she is excited, but her words just like then, could not drown out his thoughts. Carl tried to remember Pastor Matthews counseling during their sessions, but all that is blank. Carl knows it is nothing but nerves; he is having a hard time believing he is so nervous. Carl is so anxious that he has tuned out Jill. Jill for the third time says,

"Daddy…you okay?" Carl appears to pop out of a trance.

"Yes, baby girl what's up?"

"Are you okay? I know you have not heard a thing I am saying. It is as if you are in another world. Thinking about Mom in that world?"

Carl immediately disregarding her question about Jessica says, "I am good, I am good, yeah…yeah…I am good," nodded Carl.

Jill folded her arms, "Yeah right Dad, are you trying to convince me or you?" Carl did not respond, and there is a brief moment of silence.

Carl pulls in front of the wellness center in the designated registration spaces. While he is parking the car, Jill breaks the silence.

"Daddy you don't have to say a word, I know you are nervous. I don't know where you are with forgiving

Mom, and you don't owe me any type of explanation. But, I recall being so upset with Carla Goldsmith for drinking out of my favorite Coke-a-Cola glass when I was eight years old. I remember the day she dropped it and the glass broke. Out of all the glasses in the cabinet, she picked that glass to use. I was mad at her, as only an eight year old girl could be over her favorite glass..." Jill giggles. "...when she left, I just complained and complained about my glass being broke. A very wise man taught me a valuable lesson about forgiveness that day. He says, *you have to forgive Carla, because if you do something wrong and don't forgive Carla, God won't forgive you when you need him to.*"

Carl feels the tears ready to spring forth. He and Jill smile at each other and Carl says, "Baby girl..." the tears fall. "...I love you!"

Jill and Carl embrace. Jill takes a tissue from her purse and wipes her Daddy's eyes. Carl says, "Now, who needs to wipe the tears?" They both laugh.

Carl and Jill are walking toward the front door of the Wellness Center when the Concierge walks out with Jessica's bags.

"Hello Mr. Richardson, I have Mrs. Richardson's bags." Carl is going to respond to the young concierge, when he notices Jessica walking through the front door.

Jessica starts walking down the stairs. Carl feels as if time has stood still. Jessica looks amazingly beautiful. She is wearing his favorite St. John piece. The red knit skirt is hugging her curvy hips and her hair bounces with every step she takes toward him. Jessica's ankle patent strapped pump is like icing on the cake. Jessica walks right up to Carl. Carl does not move and his face looked as if his bottom lip would lower at any moment.

By her father's reaction, Jill is pleasantly stunned, but it is no doubt that her mother is looking her best, and her make-up made it all pop for sure. Jill says, "Mom I don't know who did your make-up but they beat the fool out of your face!"

Jessica's bright looking smile went to a frown and Jill quickly added, "That's slang for its THE BOMB!!" Jill hugs her mom. "I am so glad you are coming home."

Jessica happily replies, "So am I..." Jessica looks up to Carl's six foot three frame and stretches out her arms hoping he does not reject her, but based on the look on his face, she thinks, *"I will certainly get a hug, how could he resist?"*

Carl steps into Jessica's arms. Her head melts into Carl's chest. It has been so long since she felt his beating heart. His hands moving down her back makes her hold his waist tighter. In that moment, Jessica feels the only reason why the world is spinning is because Carl is the earth's axis.

Chapter Twenty-three

Henry walks in the restaurant and Pastor Matthews
motions him over to the table. Pastor Matthews and
Henry greet each other with a handshake. Henry
towers over Pastor Matthews's five-foot-six stature.
Pastor Matthews is a medium build man. His skin is a
smooth dark chocolate and has wavy salt and pepper
hair. He is just a few years older than Henry and Carl.

Pastor Matthews and Henry exchange their afternoon
greetings. Pastor Matthews sips on his coffee while
Carl orders his espresso. Pastor Matthews looks over
his wire-framed glasses and says,

"How are you doing?" The server drops off Henry's espresso. Feeling the warmth of the mug, Henry replies,

"Pastor...I am okay...I am...I don't know...I will be better when Stephanie comes home."

"So Stephanie is still in Pensacola?" says Pastor Matthews.

"Well, she flies into Pensacola, but our property is actually located in Destin. Yes, she is still there. She and Shane talk daily. I send her texts and let her know I love her. I am trying to give her the necessary space she needs. But the longer she stays away, the more I think that....that...she won't come back." A little tear trickled down from Henry's right eye. Pastor Matthews moving his coffee cup aside tells Henry,

"Oh ye of little faith...let me remind you that you shall have what you say. Henry you have to declare from your mouth that your marriage is healed. You have repented, but it sounds as if you are still riddled with guilt and haven't forgiven yourself."

Henry, sipping his espresso agrees, "Pastor you are correct. I wish I would have told her sooner and …I should have…who am I kidding? All of this shoulda – woulda – coulda…I feel so bad and want her so much, but don't want to push her away permanently… and I don't…" Pastor Matthews, who rarely interrupts Henry in their sessions, gives Henry a perplexed look and says, "Hold on! Is this the same Henry McFinley I have known all these years? No-nonsense, aggressive, former Miami U linebacker and Real-estate Developer? That same tenacity you showed on the football field, and now show in your career is still inside of you. Tap into it! The play has been called; don't let Stephanie get past you! Do you remember when we were looking for a site for our new church?" Henry acknowledges that he remembers with a head nod. Pastor Matthews continues, "You were relentless; you would fire people off our team if they weren't full of faith. You would tell me '*Pastor we can't have those wavering in faith concerning what God is trying to do with Higher Calling Christian*

Fellowship'. Therefore, Henry McFinley, I tell you this afternoon, you cannot waver in your faith concerning your relationship with your wife Stephanie. Have faith, do not go out without a fight, fight for your marriage Henry, and be relentless. Go after your wife, and don't let her get away."

Chapter Twenty-four

Selma walks back into the apartment to hear Marcie
hanging up the phone abruptly saying,

 "She is not here…sure, good-bye."

"Marcie who is that?" Marcie, not concerned with
keeping the peace, turns with her arms folded and
looks at Selma says,

"Mark Swindoll."

"Oh really…well why did you tell him I isn't here?
You know I was coming back."

Marcie with much frustration looks at her mother and
says, "Mom, I don't understand. No one knows better
than me that Daddy is a…" Marcie stops herself; she
never speaks against her father and will not start now.

"…but why didn't you just leave instead of cheating. Why did you take that risk? If he ever found out, you know that it would have been much worse!" Selma replies,

"Marcie, I haven't talked to Mr. Swindoll in months…"

Marcie interrupts, rolling her eyes up in her head, "Oh right…"

Selma, following behind Marcie to the living room, decides it is time to tell Marcie the truth.

"Marcie, please sit down. While as your mother I don't owe you an explanation…I do understand and see where my actions would be considered suspect to you. I never told you before because…well, I am not sure what I am going to do; and if I decided to move forward as Mark wanted me to…"

Marcie folding her arms tighter, says "OH Mark now!" Selma continues as if Marcie didn't say a word.

"…There is a case opened against your father concerning his transaction at the brokerage firm. It has thought he has profit from corrupt dealings. However,

Mr. Swindoll is hoping that Calvin would turn, or considering the circumstance, I would find documentation that would support the corrupt dealings...such as a ledger or any type of documentation."

Marcie's mouth drops, "Is he with the FBI?" Selma nods,
"Yes, and after I had enough nerve to tell Mr. Swindoll about the abusive situation, he agreed to work the case under cover and get as close as he could, but to no avail...finally, after you became pregnant I is ready to move full steam ahead. Authorities searched and there is nothing turned up. Your dad lost his memory and that rather blew his case. Mr. Swindoll believed that he isn't working alone, but that he is just a pawn in the game."

Marcie, still with her mouth dropped says, "I can't believe this...when will the drama end? Do you have anything else to tell me? No, no, no...don't tell me... this is one more thing I will have to process... just keep giving it to me piece by piece." Marcie, still taken aback by the story, looked at Selma wondering *"Is this really the truth?"* One thing Marcie knows is that her mother has never lied to her, and she has no reason to start now.

Marcie, going through her many questions in her head, says, "Mom, I am sorry. I know you are not my enemy. I am working through everything in counseling; at least I am trying…you probably just knocked off three weeks." Marcie jokes, hoping her mother will chuckle. Selma looks at Marcie and they both laughed. Marcie and Selma embrace.

"Marcie I love you!"
"I love you too Mommy!" Marcie lays her head in her mother's lap looking up at the ceiling, still filtering through her many questions.
"Mommy, so while we are talking…are we talking freely?" Selma looks at Marcie,
"I would say this is pretty free." Marcie asks,
"What about the red roses; what is that about?"

Selma holds her head back. She thinks she should just lay it all out on the line. Selma let out a sigh, "Well…that is the first time Mr. Swindoll had done anything like that. I couldn't remember the last time I felt such…concern…such respect. I definitely began to look at him differently. I felt it before, but immediately reminded myself that I is married, and thought he wouldn't be interested in me. Well, that day it is something else. We talked about it later and indeed, he expressed some interest, but seeing your reaction, and all that we were going through at the time, there is no way I could get involved in another relationship. I had to find out who I was."

Marcie's eyes commenced to well up. She couldn't help but think, *"Did I ruin my mother's chance of true happiness?"*
"Mommy, I am so sorry…." Selma immediately interrupts,
"Oh no Marcie Taylor, you do not have to be sorry, you are the most important person to me right now…"

Selma rubs Marcie's forehead and continues, "…if it's meant to be, it will be!" They both smile.

Chapter Twenty-five

As Stephanie walks along the beach, she answers her afternoon call with Pastor Joy, Pastor Matthews' wife. Pastor Joy is always on time. Stephanie started counseling with Pastor Joy the moment she decided to come to the beach house. Although Stephanie holds her PhD in psychology, she understands that self-counseling is not wise.

"Hello this is Stephanie."

"Hello, Stephanie, Pastor Joy here, how are you doing? I hear the ocean behind you; walking on the beach?"

"Yes, and it's a striking sight, not to mention calming."

"Stephanie, how are you doing processing your feelings concerning you and Henry?"

Pastor Joy recognized for her no nonsense, direct approach and style. She is not your typical church traditional pastor's wife. She has her own personality and style of ministry that compliments her husband well. Stephanie actually welcomes this style, which is very close to her own. She needs this *"no nonsense-in-your-face-deal-with-it."*

"Slowly…I don't have a desire to leave Henry. I just don't want to look at him…" Pastor Joy chuckled. Stephanie continues, "…I is so busy in *support* mode making sure Shane and Henry were okay, I didn't deal with my own feelings. The years of deceit caused me to question everything…and whose feelings is he considering more, Jessica's or mine? He kept her secret to be deceitful to me...his wife. Now, when I think on those lines, I get...excuse me Pastor...pissed. Then, the rational side of me says, do you know how long ago that is? I am not upset per se about the act, because it is years ago, early in our marriage while we were separated! I *am* upset about the years of lies...then...I...I also is in a situation where I could have slipped, but I didn't, so it is a matter of a decision."

"Stephanie, I understand exactly where you are. However, both of us know that you are staying away will not bring about the healing you and Henry need. When are you coming home?"
"I told Shane I would be home for graduation. I have already purchased my ticket, but it is a round trip ticket. I am not ready to stay. Pastor Joy, this may sound a little off, but I do not want to give him the chance to say anything *"stupid"*...trying to *"fix it"*. Most men are fixers I'm afraid, and that's the bottom line."

Pastor Joy, having listened intently, says to Stephanie, "Where you are right now, I refer to as the *zone of intolerance*. When a woman is in that zone, anything is liable to trigger the emotion of anger, if not rage, by one act of *"stupid."* Stephanie laughs and says, "I like that terminology. I will adopt it into my repertoire." They both laugh.

"Seriously, that zone of intolerance is birthed from our flesh. I've been there individually, and I have been there with my husband. He preaches from our life together, we have faced many intense fellowships; there is a time that is so intense that like you, I had to steal away. I didn't think that it is a deal breaker, but I didn't want to look at him. Thank God, we didn't have any children, so my decision is easier and I felt as if it isn't hurting anyone. However, that is not true because everyone connected to us is affected by our decisions. Romans tells us that we cannot please God in our flesh."

As Stephanie's tears fell, she moves her feet back and forth in the sand.

"I know… I need God to move on my heart to rekindle that spark that drew me to Henry. I need God to touch that place in my heart that needs to forgive so I am not stuck on what has happened, but what can happen with God as the center of our joy."

Chapter Twenty-six

Jill and Jessica talk all the way home. Jessica tries to engage Carl in conversation, but once again, his thoughts are consuming him. Jessica even at one point tries to hold Carl's hand. While that snaps him out of daze, it is only long enough to move away from Jessica.

Once home, Carl carries in Jessica's bags and takes them to their bedroom. Jill continues to monopolize her time by continuing their girl talk in the family room. Carl stays upstairs until Jill calls for him. "Daddy where are you, come on down." Carl comes down.

"There you are. Thank you so much for my roses..." says Jessica. There on the counter were four dozen of the most beautifully arranged yellow roses. Each rose made a perfect bloom. Jessica continues, "...Carl they are absolutely gorgeous. Thank you, thank you so much."

Carl immediately turns to Jill, knowing that he did not order the roses. Jill looks at her father and gives him *the look* so Carl replies. "You're welcome Jessica." Carl smiles.

Jessica returns the favor. She is sitting on the sofa with her legs crossed. She did not take off her pumps. She is sitting talking with Jill, moving her leg up and down as she normally does when she crosses them. As much as he tries, he does not want to stare but, Jessica's beauty is the driving force. Carl is so attracted to her, not in a lustful matter. He cannot identify exactly what it is but Carl thought, *"Whatever it is, I like it..."* Just then, the doorbell rings. Carl thought *"...saved by the bell."*

Carl turns quickly to answer the door. There stands Henry and Shane with roses. Carl cannot believe it…he guesses he had not noticed Shane's growth spurt. Shane walks in the door with flowers and open arms.

"Hey, Uncle Carl, what's up my man?!" Carl smiles "Man, you have grown. Henry what are you feeding this boy?"
Henry laughs, "He's not eating any more than usual. It must be the love bug." Carl and Henry laugh and greet each other just like old times with their special handshake and a one-arm hug. It is a natural response and they both simultaneously realize what had just happened and hug each other again with two arms.

Shane runs into the family room "Aunt Jess!" Jessica, in bewilderment, stood up and says,
"Oh my goodness! Shane you are so tall. Jill, you forgot to tell me that little fact." Shane picks Jessica up,

"Shane, put me down…" Jill chimes in,
"Yes, that is his favorite thing to do to now, pick everybody up." Everyone laughs.

Shane has a dozen of red roses arranged like most pageant bouquets. He says, "Aunt Jess these are for you…nothing like Uncle Carl's…" Shane looks over at the four dozen spread, "…but we are glad you are home too." Jessica kisses Shane and says,
"Thank you, love. It is appreciated and I am more than happy to be home. I have waited some time for this…and….and…" Jessica starts to cry. Jill immediately stands and hugs her mom. Jessica patting her eyes with the back of her hand went to put her roses in water.

Shane walks to Jill and hugs her as if he hasn't seen her in months. Shane kisses Jill on her cheek and says,
"For you my sweetness…" He pulled from his jacket pocket a gift.
"What is this Shane?"

"Open it." Jill removes the meticulously wrapped chocolate gift-wrap and opens the long jewelry case. "Oh Shane…"

It is the gold charm bracelet with a single charm engraved with the day's date and inscribed with *"New Beginnings, Love Shane"*. Shane knows how special this day is to Jill to have her mom home.

"Thanks Shane" This time, it is Jill that is initiating the kissing.

This is Jessica's first experience with Jill and Shane kissing. She walks in stunned and Jessica looks at Carl and Henry as if *"everyone okay with this?"* Carl and Henry both say,

"I know, I know." Henry greets Jessica with a hug and welcomes her home. Jessica having no idea but stating the obvious says,
"Stephanie decided to stay home?" Stephanie had visited and sent cards, but she had not seen her in

several weeks. She never asks Carl about it. Everyone including Shane and Jill look at Henry with sympathetic eyes.

"Uhm...uhm..." Henry looks to Carl for guidance and Carl nods his head, giving permission to proceed. "Stephanie needs some time alone and she went to the beach property in Destin." Jessica, looking down could not help but wonder *"have I lost my best, long time friend forever?"*

Shane, the master of conversation steering jokingly says, "So Aunt Jess, you didn't expect your nephew to be this fine did you?" Jill hits Shane on his shoulder, everyone shakes their head.

"Oh please Shane McFinley, I changed your dirty diapers boy."

"Ah Aunt Jess, you didn't have to go there." They laugh.

Carl watches Jessica as she walks back to the couch, he feels as if she has some type of spell on him. He

thinks *"God is this you working it out?"* Carl turns to
Henry and says,

"Hey man let's go out back."

Henry, closing the glass patio door behind him, says
"Carl, how are you doing man?" Carl chuckles and
shook his head says,

"Man, I don't know. My feelings are so mixed. I have
been praying for God to change my heart and man she
walked out the door…when I looked up at her…man,
I froze. You see her? She looks *good*!" Carl looked at
Henry as if to say, *you know she does*. Henry says,

"I am scared to respond…" Carl laughs,

"I know man, you're trying to feel what bag I am
going to come out of …" Carl pats Henry on his
shoulder and they both give a quick smile. Carl
continues,

"…Henry let's put this behind us. I am not going to be
able to work this out without you man. During
Jessica's counseling sessions, she answered all of my
questions and she told me you wanted to come clean.
She is actually afraid that you would because she

thought there is no way you were going to be able to hold this from me. So, God is able to deal with me quickly concerning you." Henry, with a tear stricken face says,

"Man I wanted to call you so many times. I wanted to talk to you so bad. Stephanie leaving is really taking a toll on me. I do not know whether to let her have her space or fly to Pensacola to get her. If I could have talked to you, I probably would have flown up there yesterday. Henry, looking a little surprised contains his composure. Just as if he is in the courtroom and surprised by witness testimony he says,

"Well Henry, the one thing I know about Stephanie, she still loves you. You need to fight for her. You know, you were unstoppable when you first met her, and she has someone pursuing her intensely. That didn't stop you; you were there for her… for every little thing. Remember she told you it was your honesty that drew her…it will be your honesty that draws her back. Let her know how you feel."

Carl and Henry embrace. Henry smiles and says, "Thanks man, it's good to have your advice back. So, are you taking the same advice to fight?" Carl held his head down.

"Man…" Carl walks toward one of the patio chairs and sits down. "…I know she wants this to work, I am trying to get past the deceit…and for so long. You know how I feel about my baby girl, that's really it. The thought that she possibly…" Henry interrupts, "Man stop reliving it…I am trying to take that same advice." Carl and Henry continue their conversation for hours like old times, with more tears and laughter that the whole house can hear.

Jessica slid the patio door open and says, "Hey boys, do you see the time?" Henry immediately jumps up, thinking that Carl and Jessica need some *"alone"* time says, "Oh wow, later man, Shane and I will be going." Henry walks back into the house. Carl is right behind him, but Jessica reaches out for Carl and holds him by his arm.

"Carl I am so glad to be home…home with Jill and with you." She lays her head on his arm. Carl ran his fingers through the back of Jessica's hair and walks into the house.

Jill runs to the patio door, gives her father and mother both good night greetings. Jill took a bottle of water out of the refrigerator and says,
"Don't forget Shane and I are going to Courtney's wedding tomorrow, so I will probably not be around for a while. You two enjoy!" Jessica smiles at Jill as she left the family room.

Carl grabs an apple off the kitchen island and starts to eat it. Jessica and Carl are alone for the first time, and Jessica does not know how Carl will respond. She notices how he is behaving, but she does not if he is being cordial for Jill's sake, or what.
"Carl, do you want to watch a movie?" Carl responds as if he is dealing with a business associate says, "No, I am going to retire for the evening. I have placed your bags in our..." he caught himself, "…in your

bedroom. I will take the guest room upstairs." Carl, having devoured the apple, throws it away.

Jessica throwing all caution to the wind wraps her arms around Carl's waist says,
"Carl, let's talk, honey... I have missed you...missed you so much, I have slept alone for the past six months. I am home and I do not want to sleep without you next to me. I just want to hold you...feel you next to me." Carl unable to resist the heat of Jessica's body wraps his enormous arms around Jessica's petite structure. Carl returns her embrace, which causes Jessica's heart to race with hope of acceptance to her invitation. Rubbing his hands through her hair, he whispers,
"Jess, just give me some more time."

Chapter Twenty-seven

Shane and Jill settle into their seats at the wedding
right up front. Marcie is Courtney's bridal attendant.
She asks the coordinator to make sure Shane and Jill
have seats. The chapel is beautiful. It smells of the
hundreds of Ecuador roses displayed in two large
arrangements on the pulpit, and the arrangement of
roses and lilies around the single candelabras that
flank every other pew down the center aisle. Each pew
is also finished with yards of white shimmering tulle
held in place with the most elaborate wired pink
organza bows. The center aisle covers with pink
iridescent rose petals sparkled at every guest as they
walk into the chapel. The chapel fills quickly

prompting church members to give up their seats so John's family can sit down.

Shane joked throughout the whole service until the wedding march played and Courtney entered the chapel center aisle. Courtney is stunning. She wears a white form fitting beaded strapless gown with a three-foot train. Her flowers were a small bouquet of pink peonies and roses accented with white gardenias. John rambles in French,

"Ceci est ma beauté...l'amour de ma vie" the moment she appears at the top of the center aisle.

Courtney stands at top of the aisle thinking to herself *"What in the world am I doing?"* Every dark and painful detail of her past passes through her mind. Before she knows it, she walks to the altar and wipes John's tears from his cheeks. Courtney carefully listens to the vows and thinks to herself, *"Could he really... for better or worse...could she really for better or worse, what if he hadn't told her everything..."* Courtney dismisses that thought; she knows that John is always open with her. She is the one who getting information from is like pulling teeth.

As quickly as it begins, it ends; so it appears to Courtney. She and John are pronounced husband and wife.

Chapter Twenty-eight

Carl, rubbing his eyes, went to move when he realizes, Jessica is in the bed lying at his feet. His heart melts. Jessica is a very matter of fact person, and if she thinks she is right, she will hold her ground. Jessica and Carl have slept apart only one other time in their marriage and that is when she found out that he was having an affair with Beverly Martinez. As hurt and upset as she was, Carl can never forget when he woke up to find Jessica at his feet just like now…as Ruth lay at Boaz's feet indicating she is ready for marriage.

There is such an aromatic smell in the room. Jessica lit candles. Jessica has a CD playing. It is Pastor Matthews's message on marriage. Carl slowly moves from under the blankets hoping not to disturb Jessica;

she looks so peaceful. She lay at Carl's feet facing him as if she has fallen asleep watching him. Carl moves to the foot of the bed gently caressing Jessica's hair; he smiles to himself because she did not put her nightcap on. She knows he loves running his hands through her hair. Carl moves closer to Jessica under the blanket she has brought from the other room. He pulls himself to her, being ever careful not to disturb her sleep. When he settles in his place to hold Jessica, he hears an unconscious sigh. Jessica's eyes are puffy and swollen. Carl knows she must have been crying most of the night.

As his tears fall, he continues to caress her hair and then her face. He kisses her eyes wishing each kiss would bury her pain. Carl knows that in that moment God is indeed touching his heart because all he is concerned about is protecting and loving Jessica.

Jessica wakes up to Carl moving his hand down her arm and then he movs under her silk pajama shirt to rub the small of her back. When she opens her eyes Carl says,

"What God has joined together…" Jessica finishes "…let no man put asunder." Carl rolles Jessica over on him and he holds and kisses her.

After lying in the bed for the next thirty minutes in complete silence and just holding each other, Carl asks,

"Do you want to go out for breakfast? Lunch? or whatever the meal is. What time is it?" Jessica giggles like a schoolgirl.

"Sure, I will run your bath water… in our Jacuzzi." Carl smiles and kisses her forehead.

Jessica finishes dressing and decides to put her things away when she notices that Carl also has a duffle bag, as if he has been away. She grabs the bag to put his things up. When she opens the bag an 8 ½ x 11 envelope sits on top with his name on the front. Jessica thinks that the hand writing looks familiar and remembers her mail from Rose Farland.

Carl is getting dressed when he thinks he smells something burning. He attempts initially to ignore it but he continues to smell it. He calls out "Jessica…hey babe…Jessica what's burning?" A little more concerned with her not answering, Carl finishes buttoning his shirt as he makes his way to the family room.

There, Jessica sits in front of the fireplace holding the 8 ½ x 11 envelope that he has found on his windshield at the airport. She has two additional envelopes; he thinks, *"Where did those come from? Oh God, did Beverly send those pictures to Jessica while she was in Rose Farland?"* Carl could feel his heart racing. He didn't know what Jessica is going to think. Hopefully, this will not cause her to relapse and she knows that they are old pictures. Carl is frustrated with himself, because he should have followed his first mind and taken the pictures to the office. Anxiously, Carl calls, "Jessica..." Jessica didn't reply. Carl decides right then, there is no need to start all over with any secrets;

he is also going to tell her about the weekend. Carl walks right up behind Jessica; she has the envelopes lying in her lap.

"Jessica I don't want any secrets between us, if we are going to start over let's do it right. I have an idea where that envelope came from, but you have to know that…" Jessica holds up her hand. Carl isn't sure exactly what her hand gesture means. Jessica stands up and turns to Carl.

"Carl I agree with you and we shouldn't." Jessica turns and threw the envelopes into the fire. Jessica turns back to Carl to hold him. "Carl, the past is the past." Carl, tremendously relieved, holds Jessica tight. "I will handle that, first thing next week…" Carl pulls Jessica away from her. He looks into her eyes and says,
"There is something else I need to tell you about…regarding a trip I took…" Jessica holds up her hand again and says,
"Carl, the past is the past."

Chapter Twenty-nine

Beverly orders her favorite eggs Benedict drizzled with hollandaise sauce and garlic potatoes on a bed of sautéed spinach and onions. Her glass of mimosa she sipps, leaving her signature Dior lipstick ring. Beverly is casually dressed in a Navy DK pantsuit and a pair of flat patent Stuart Weitzman shoes. Beverly sits musing over the next phase of her plan concerning Carl Richardson when Caleb walks up.

"Well, fancy meeting you here, Beverly Martinez."

"Hello Caleb, yes, fancy meeting you here." Beverly isn't terribly disturbed that Caleb notices her because she could easily dismiss him or just hope he is meeting someone else for brunch. Caleb makes his move, as she fears he would.

"So, may I join you for brunch, or do you have someone else joining you?"

Just as Beverly is going to let Caleb down easy, her eyes cannot believe what she is seeing. Beverly thinks, *"Is it possible for this morning to become anymore interesting?"* Carl and Jessica come through the door of Johnny's Bistro. Beverly immediately motions Caleb to have a seat.

"No Caleb, I don't have anyone joining me please...please join me." Caleb, with a high-school boy's grin sits right down. The opportunity to spend time with Beverly turns his nightly fantasies into reality. Beverly giving no thought to Caleb's increasing level of excitement, discreetly keeps her eye on Carl and Jessica. Beverly engages Caleb just enough to keep his focus on her; so he will not notice her gliding attention toward the seemingly joyous Richardsons.

As Beverly and Caleb complete their meals, she secretly is regretting that Caleb spotted her in the restaurant. Of all the restaurants on the city's historical restaurant row, Caleb had to select Johnny's Bistro. The waiter removing the last of their dishes asks if there is anything else. Caleb trying to show initiative told the waiter that he is taking care of the check. Beverly rolled her eyes in her head and thinks *"How uncouth, he should have says it will be one check."* The waiter politely acknowledges Caleb and left to prepare the bill. As the waiter opens up the line of sight to the Richardsons, Beverly is able to see Carl leave the table going to the rest room. Caleb nervously excuses himself from Beverly to do the same. Beverly seizes the occasion to make her move.

Beverly grabs her handbag and moves as quickly as possible with Jessica in her sight. Without a plan, Beverly knows she has to think rapidly. Beverly, uncharacteristically with a high pitch voice, says "Mrs. Richardson.... Jessica is that you?" With just as much surprise, Jessica stands and hugs Beverly and says, "Hello Beth, what are the chances that we would meet here?" Beverly continuing, "I know….I wish I would have seen you earlier, I just ate alone. Are you alone as well?"

"Oh no, my husband and I are enjoying a lovely morning together. I am so happy to be home and spend some much needed time with my family." Beverly replies with the unseen malice in her heart and knowing she doesn't have much time,

"Oh, Jessica that is just great. Let's have lunch sometime…of course after you have spent that much needed time with your family."
Jessica with a slight smiles says, "How about we get together tomorrow morning before church service? My family will not be coming, so I would love the company." Beverly, caught off guard by Jessica's invitation doesn't readily accept, but Jessica insisted, and in an effort not to spoil her cover and to move out of the restaurant before Caleb or Carl returns, Beverly finally agrees. Jessica and Beverly confirm their cell

phone numbers. Jessica suggests that they meet there at Johnny's for breakfast and then go to service together.

Beverly eagerly wishing to leave Jessica says, "Tomorrow, it's a date!" and Beverly hugs Jessica and plants a *"Judas"* kiss on her cheek. Jessica smiles and says,
"Beth, it will be great to spend time with you tomorrow." Beverly quickly made her way out of the bistro.

Jessica smiles as she thinks about how she and Beth met at Rose Farland. Beth is always so pleasant to her and she cannot forget her lovely gift basket. Carl interrupts her thoughts as he returns to the table with a look of disdain. Jessica with a paranoid concern asks, "Honey what's wrong?" Carl did not respond, as he quickly scans the restaurant. Jessica, growing increasingly more uncomfortable presses Carl for a response.

"Carl, what is it honey?" Carl still very much distracted, continues to look around the restaurant expecting the familiar fragrance to be matched with Beverly's face. Carl replies,

"Nothing, honey…well, I have an uneasy feeling. Is there anyone here at the table that appears to behave strangely?" Jessica's thoughts all ran together with her intuition heightened but answers nonetheless,

"No one but a young lady named Beth who does outreach work at Rose Farland. She is having brunch here in the restaurant. You will have the opportunity to meet her tomorrow, I invited her to church and we are going to have brunch here tomorrow before service."

Carl's worst fear is realized and anxiously states, "What?...Do you know anything about this woman? I don't think…" To Carl's surprise, Jessica is calm, and interrupts, "Carl, don't worry honey, I know more about this woman than even she thinks."

Chapter Thirty

It is another beautiful day on the beach. Stephanie takes her customary seat on the deck of the house. The smell of her coffee and the ocean's salt is her morning aromatic treat. The sounds of the sea gulls give her comfort and confirmation of life on earth. The daybreak tides are subsiding and the morning sun begins its position for its afternoon blaze.

Stephanie lifts her coffee mug and admires her daily sounds and scents. She lays her head back on the lounge chair. Stephanie is relaxing without one care in the world or remembrance of her current life. Her existing state of reality is shocked when her cell phone rings. Stephanie did not move in hopes that the irritant would somehow cease to exist. However, Stephanie could no longer ignore the ring for it is an all too familiar sound. She only looks at her cell phone display out of habit. She knows that it is Henry calling. This is the one time she is regretting assigning Henry a special ring.

Stephanie reminded her reality the instant her cell phone rings Not having the desire to speak with Henry, Stephanie put her coffee mug down and runs toward the beach.

Stephanie jumps in the water in hopes that the tide would take away her disappointment. Unfortunately, the tide pushes up memories of her life with Henry. Stephanie lying on her back in the ocean is feeling the waves gently rocking her and bringing comfort to her broken heart.

As hard as Stephanie tries to forget Henry, the thoughts of him continues to bombard her. Stephanie can count on Henry always being there for her during her low moods. Henry would hold her and give her a private recital. Stephanie reminisces on the first time she learned of Henry's vocal abilities. After losing her mother, she recalls feeling as if she was all alone during her sophomore year of college. Expressing that to Henry, to Stephanie's surprise a smooth, rich tenor rendition of "You Will Never Walk Alone" soothed her grief.

Stephanie quietly begins to sing the song to herself all the while envisioning Henry singing in her ear. Her tears start to roll down the side of her face. She decides that she will not stop the tears from falling this time. Stephanie finally releases her tears, which cannot be distinguished from the ocean, for they both now are one.

Chapter Thirty-one

Shane, Jill and Marcie give their good-byes and warm wishes to Courtney and John. John is happy as he twirls his bride around. John and Courtney continue to wave through their limo sunroof. Guests continue to wave until they are out of sight.

Shane turns to Jill, "Hey Jill, you ready?"
Jill says "Yes, but…" Jill interrupts her own thought and says,

"Hey Marcie you want to hang out with us?" Marcie rolling her eyes in her head says,

"Oh, no I am not interested in being the third wheel, besides…" Marcie grabs her stomach "…I have been on my feet enough. There is my mom now, you love birds have fun." Marcie gives her hugs and telss Jill she will call her later. Jill replies,

"Yes, we will talk about what we are going to wear to graduation!" They all smile. Shane and Jill wave to Selma.

Shane places his hand around Jill's waist, pulls her to himself, and says, "Well, it appears Ms. Richardson I have you all to myself, or would you rather go home and spend some time with your mom? I won't be that selfish to keep you the rest of the day." Jill wraps her arms around Shane's neck and smiles,

"I do want to be with my mom, but I believe her and my dad, need their time. I am hoping that they are taking that opportunity now. You are so considerate Shane McFinley!"

"I aim to please…so where do you want to go? How about we walk along the river?" Shane and Jill start walking to the car hand in hand. Jill says, "That would be great."

Shane opens the car door for Jill. After getting in the car, Jill suddenly moves into her private world of thought. She begins to reflect on the whirlwind her life has taken the past six months. Attending the wedding also made her think about her new found relationship with Shane. Jill and Shane always discuss everything, but she has held back discussing their relationship as graduation approaches, due to his mom leaving.

They arrive at the city's renovated river walk. Families and couples alike were out enjoying the last of the day's sun as dusk is quickly approaching. Shane opens the door for Jill and extends his hand to help her out of the car. Shane thinks Jill is beautiful with her rhinestone encrusted silver sandals that accompanied a spaghetti strapped, salmon colored, A-line laced dress with a scalloped hem that hits just above Jill's knees. Jill catches Shane looking at her in his boyish admiration, but she wants to shift his attention. There is yet another topic that they have yet to address,

"So, Shane, tell me how are you really feeling about your mom being gone this long?"Shane's countenance takes an apparent shift but he remains engaged with Jill by holding her hand.

"I am…I can't lie and say I am alright. I am ready for her to come home. I believe God that she will be home to stay when she comes for graduation. I purposely keep myself in that state so I am not consumed. You know this is all new to me. My parents had disagreements, but I never experienced anything like this so that's makes it hard for me…." Shane pauses and kisses Jill on her hand.

"…you know… having you makes it easier…"

Jill smiles and before she realizes she has spoken thoughts that she hidden for weeks.

"…yeah but what happens when you go away to school?" Jill immediately bows her head thinking to herself *"Oh my God, Jill you said that out loud!"* Shane losing his grip on Jill's hand says, "What? What do you mean what happens? Have you changed your plans to attend Stanford and haven't told me?"

Jill, unable to retract her untimely outburst says, "I have been entertaining the idea of staying closer to home and maybe going to Hampton." Shane completely caught off guard is silent. Jill knew as Shane slips his hand away from hers that he has just disconnected. In an attempt to recover, Jill says, "I didn't say anything because of what is going on with Uncle Henry and Aunt Stephanie, my mom and dad and I know how much you have always wanted to go to Stanford. I don't want to be the reason you…." Shane interrupts,

"Jill, I hear you, but I held my decision in hopes of not being on one coast and you on the other. We have constantly talked about this, and now…for you to drop this….”

“I haven’t… I didn’t say I was going, I was…”

“I know what you said Jill, and for you to entertain the thought, it’s a greater possibility than you admit, and for you not to tell me!…” Jill interrupts,

“…well I definitely didn’t expect this reaction!”

Shane stops walking and leans over the overlook railing. Jill can not translate Shane’s pointless stare. A little more irritated, Shane replies,

“Well…what did you expect? You just blurted this out apparently unintentionally,” Jill, definitely startled by Shane’s interruption, says,

“Okay, you are right, but I think that we should…”

Shane sternly says,

“We should do what?”

Chapter Thirty-two

Henry spends most of the day worshipping and reading his Word only taking breaks to call Stephanie several times. Unfortunately, she refuses to answer his call. Today during his study time, Henry feels a sense of relief and breaking. Self-pity parties and frantic expectations of Stephanie returning home fills his weekends.

Henry is charging his faith with the Word of God, believing what good thing God had started He is faithful to complete. Henry knows that includes his marriage to Stephanie.

At the end of the day, Henry retires to the master bedroom where he intends on continuing his night in worship. He figures Shane will not be in until later in the evening. Henry hits the remote to the stereo. David and Nicole Binion's "Heaven on Earth" saturates the atmosphere.

Henry starts the water in the Jacuzzi, but decides he will reserve that for when Stephanie returns home. He opts for a shower instead. Henry, in the middle of his shower, thinks he hears his cell phone ring. He quickly rinses and darts for his phone wet from head to toe. All Henry could think, *"It could be Stephanie calling."* Henry catches the phone on the last ring. Unfortunately, to his dissatisfaction, he is dismissing a caller with the wrong number.

Henry continues to think about Stephanie, but decides another call is not fruitful. She obviously needs more time. Henry lowering the volume on the stereo and did what is becoming his nightly ritual. From the bedside nightstand, he takes Stephanie's hand held recorder and plays her memos back.

Henry listens, not to invade her privacy, but to hear Stephanie's voice. He sits on her side of the bed and closeshis eyes to envision her in his mind, wishing all the time that it is actually her standing there. To Henry's surprise when he pushes the play button Stephanie's next memo is, *"Vow renewal song ideas, Brian McKnight's latest CD Evolution of a Man."*

Henry stops the recorder and jumps up to find the CD Stephanie is referring too. He isn't surprised because Stephanie loves Brian McKnight and most love ballads. Henry flips through their CD cases. All the other Brian McKnight CD's were there, with the exception of the one Stephanie mentions. Henry continues his search. The CD has fallen behind the player. Henry opens the case and there is a small post-it listing track numbers. Henry sits in the sitting area as he listens to Stephanie's selections. The words were so appropriate for his feelings toward her. The tears commence to fall and Henry whispers,

"Stephanie I miss you!"

Chapter Thirty-three

Beverly's mind is racing as she prepares her clothes for tomorrow morning. She is still in amazement that Jessica has invited her to breakfast, and of all places church!

Beverly cannot remember the last time she attended a church service. If she has attended a service, it is some political move or the one time she wanted to watch Carl from a distance. Beverly starts to talk to herself, *"Beverly should you just do breakfast or should you actually go to church? What if someone recognizes you? Uhm, think about that girl, your plan will go up in smoke!"*

Beverly continues to ponder when her cell phone rings. The caller ID surprises her. "This is Beverly...hello, and I am surprised to hear from you...I thought you would be long gone on your week escapade... I know you are not trying to steal a moment away on your wedding night..." Beverly throwing her hair behind her ears laughed. "...I am sure it will be nothing like our week away, but you just try to enjoy....see you soon!"

Beverly immediately refocuses and tries to select clothing that Beth would wear. It is difficult for Beverly to dress down, it just isn't in her.

Beverly thinks, "*Jessica is helping me unfold my plan faster than I had anticipated, and that is good! The faster I get in, the faster I can work that Martinez magic. Carl is going to pay, one way or the other.*"

Chapter Thirty-four

Carl and Jessica came through the house laughing and licking the last of their ice cream cones. Out all day enjoying each other. They talk and laugh like college kids.

Jessica jokes, "I can't remember the last time I have been out all day and didn't return with a couple of bags." Carl snickers, "Yes and our bank account, says thank you, our closets say thank you and your already crowed 25x 25 personal walk in says thank you."

Jessica, grabs her bottom lip with her teeth and smiles as Carl is referring to their home with a plural pronoun. Jessica is glad to be home and grateful that Carl appears to be feeling the same way.

As they walk toward the family room, Carl grabs Jessica by her waist and pulls her toward him and her around. She holds his massive arms for balance. "So Mrs. Richardson, would you like to watch a movie with me?" Jessica is unable to answer and she stares into Carl's hazel colored eyes as his dark skinned serves as a complimentary backdrop. Carl says,
"Jessica, are you alright?"
 "Yes, and yes a movie would be great." Jessica finally replies, as her smile appears to be permanently plastered on her face.

Henry smiles at Jessica and runs his hand through the back of her hair. She closes her eyes in anticipation of Carl's lips gliding across her neck. She is not disappointed Carl does just that. Carl finishes by kissing Jessica on the forehead, and then leads her downstairs to their in-house movie theater.

They watched hours of Tyler Perry's *Madea* movies, laughing to the point of tears, as if it was the first time they saw the movies. Jessica yawnsand says, "Carl, we have church in the morning, let's go to bed." Carl agrees. Turning off the projector and lights, Carl and Jessica walk hand in hand up the stairs.

Carl gives Jessica a kiss on her cheek and tells her, "Good night!" Carl proceeds to walk up the steps to the guest room. After walking midway up, the staircase, with a smile, Carl turns to see Jessica still watching him and says, "Jessica, I really enjoyed our time together today, sweetie!" Jessica returns the smile and says, "I did too!"

Carl continues his climb up the steps, Jessica calling him stops him again.

"Carl…."

"Yeah sweetie?"

"Uhmm…see you tomorrow."

Carl replies, "See you tomorrow….and Jessica, I love you." Jessica's smile is even bigger as she turns to go into her bedroom.

Jessica, laying her clothes out for her breakfast with Beth, is extremely excited about her day with Carl. She wondered, off and on throughout the day, if Carl could ever forgive her. She hopes that today is a strong indication that they were definitely on the mend.

§

While Carl is undressing, he is reminiscing on his day with his lovely wife, as he moves across the room he recalls why he is sleeping in the guest bedroom. Carl rubs his left hand across his face trying to erase the tape that is playing in his head. He does not want the day to in ruins by his inability to deal with his emotions. Carl begins to pray. Clearly and quickly, he hears the answer, *"Forgive her…the day won't be ruined if you forgive."*

Carl, without hesitation and with his clothes in the floor, puts on his robe and moves down the stairs to the master bedroom. To his surprise, the bedroom door is open. Standing outside the bedroom, Carl knocks, not as a stranger, but a respectful suitor.

Jessica came to the door in her silk robe. As their eyes met, Carl never says a word. He runs his hand through Jessica's hair and with one gentle swoop, he picks her up and crosses over the thresh hold. Carl completes his knight and shining swoop with a zealous kiss that sends a tickle up the side of Jessica's leg. Carl is standing over the bed when he separates from the fiery kiss with his wife. Jessica with tears in her eyes, starts to speak, but Carl politely says,

"Shh…..I forgive you!" Carl wipes the tear from Jessica's face and lays her in the middle of their custom California king bed. He removes her robe.

Jessica is wearing a see-through white pleated, baby doll, mid-thigh gown. Carl, removing his robe loves and ravishes Jessica as if there is never a separation. They both spoke words of admiration, apologies, and love. After Carl kisses every inch of Jessica's body, they both were ready. Carl settles into Jessica, consummating his forgiveness.

Chapter Thirty-five

Beverly woke up in a cold sweat and breathing deeply. She took several moments to look around and get her bearings. Beverly is shaking by the dream, that she snatches her cell phone to see the date and time. As she looks at the time, an alert pops up on her cell phone, reminding her about her breakfast this morning with Jessica Richardson. Beverly immediately drops the phone in the bed and let out a scream as her house phone rings simultaneously. After the third ring, Beverly answers the phone still obviously shaking and in a slight panic.

"Hello…morning….Oh I…I don't know…I am okay, I think…I just had a…" Beverly is now pacing back and forth in her bedroom, rubbing her hands nervously through her hair and over her face. "…I had a dream…a dream that has me thinking…we probably shouldn't talk….I am sorry, I don't know if I can talk about…" Beverly begins to cry and she is shaking all over. "….I am going to be okay…and I do mean that we shouldn't talk anymore. You have your life and…and you should live that happy life you have with the one that really loves you….Yes…yes…yes the dream has everything to do with it….it is my mother, she is in my dream and she told me…" Beverly completely breaks down in tears. "….she told me, *stop ruining other people's lives…..and….and… more importantly stop ruining your own.* Then, she closed her eyes and died, just as she did nine years ago. So…I didn't listen then…." Beverly continues to cry and use her sheets to wipe her face. "…I think I should listen now…so take care…good-bye."

Beverly falls on her knees by the side of the bed continuing her hellacious cries of sorrow, guilt and shame. After forty-five minutes, Beverly felt like she didn't have another tear in her body. She stands under the shower for another twenty minutes, bombarded by thoughts of her dream. As she is drying off, her cell phone rings, "Hello....what's wrong? Oh God...Oh God no...this is what momma is talking about...she was in my dreams this morning...I am on the way..."

Beverly grabs her luggage and begins to pack feverously, as the tears she thinks are depleted, come rushing down her face. She grabs her keys, wipes her face once again, and says aloud, *"God it's been a long time since I have talked to you, but don't take my baby boy Carl's life....please take mine instead."* Beverly takes her keys and leaves everything behind once again, this time in hopes that the consequences of her life have not caught up with her.

Chapter Thirty-six

Jessica sits at the table at Johnny's Bistro for over forty-five minutes calling Beth, looking for an explanation for her wait. Beth does not answer the phone. It just rings.

Sipping the last of her coffee, she tells her server she does not think that her guest will be joining her this morning. Therefore, she orders her breakfast and asks for a refill on her coffee.

Jessica, tapping her fingers on the table, talks to the Lord silently *"God I know nothing happens by accident and Beth, or should I say Beverly, not showing today isn't an accident. So, I thank you for watching over me and assuring me that you have my back and revenge is yours."* Jessica smiles and immediately dismisses Beth from her thoughts concentrating only on enjoying the atmosphere of the bistro. However, that enjoyment causes her to think about her life-long friend Stephanie. She thinks about how she would have been at the table *"having her back"*.

Jessica, laughing to herself, tries to call Stephanie, who hasn't answered any of the calls since she left for the beach house. Jessica's food arrives and she blesses it and prays for her best friend to return to her and her family's life.

Chapter Thirty-seven

The praise team is in high worship when the usher escorts Jessica next to Carl. Carl with every bit of concern whispers,

"Everything okay? Are you okay?" Jessica kisses Carl on the check and whisperes,

"God does all things well! Yes...yes...yes everything is okay."

Carl hesitantly returns his focus back to worship. He is very concerned about Jessica's morning date.

Although he has no proof, he couldn't help but think Beverly is working on some destructive scheme. He knows that is her signature fragrance he smelled at the restaurant. However, Jessica's immediate thrust into worship compelled Carl to do the same.

After an hour and a half of intense worship, Pastor Matthews takes the podium and says,
"What a presence, and what an awesome atmosphere for the Word of God! So, we will hold off on announcements and offering…is that alright? Is it alright if we follow God and what he wants to do in this atmosphere?"

The congregation erupts in praise and admiration of the Lord. "Hallelujahs", "Thank you Lord" and sounds of agreement ring all throughout the sanctuary. Even the youth were on their feet encouraging Pastor Matthews to preach the Word.

Pastor Matthews excitedly began to exhort the people. As he encourages, he never opens his bible nor looks at his prepared notes. He declares the Word of the Lord based on the time he has spent with God reading his word.

Young people, children and adults alike without prompting begin to come to the altar. As the people came, Pastor Matthews starts to lay hands on the people. As the power of God moves over the congregation, several people collapse in the Spirit at the altar. Others took off running around the sanctuary or dance in praise to God.

As Pastor Matthews wipes the sweat from his brow, his wife on the altar steps meets him. She whispers in his ear and he grabs her hand. They both begin to leap and dance. The ushers and altar workers move swiftly to ensure they can assist, since they were both dancing on one-step of the altar. What a remarkable sight! It appears that the congregation gets even louder in praise as they notice their leaders worshiping and praising God.

Pastor Matthews says, "My wife just shared with me that she wants every married or engaged couple of Higher Calling Christian Fellowship to come to the altar. We are going to serve notice to saten that we are aware of his devises to destroy the family." Pastor Joy took the mic, "As your people come….. God, I declare and decree that no weapon formed against them will prosper…"

Carl takes Jessica's hand and to make their way to the altar. As they are coming down the aisle, Carl spots Henry still sitting in his seat bent over with his elbows on his knees. Carl places his hand on Henry's shoulder just as Pastor Joy says,

"… I plead the blood over unforgiveness, malice and spite. We declare today that every marriage will be made whole… for one can chase a thousand, but two can put ten thousand to flight…"

Henry stands, he and Carl hug. Henry hugs Jessica with her tear stricken face. Henry runs to the altar falling on his knees with Carl and Jessica beside him. They all three cry out to God in this moment of healing and restoration. Pastors Matthew and Joy lay their hands on Carl and Jessica, and they both hit the ground. Henry is next, and the same thing happens. It All three laying there, under the power of God, believing in faith that God will restore that which is lost.

Chapter Thirty-eight

The cell phone immediately went to voicemail. Henry is calling Stephanie without success for the past two hours. He decides to call one more time; Shane's graduation is starting in five minutes. Henry arrives back to his seat, obviously disappointed. Carl looks up at his friend and immediately knew.

"So, Stephanie didn't answer the phone? Don't worry, it's Shane's graduation. She promised to be here." Jessica, just as confident replies,

"Henry, you know Stephanie...she wouldn't disappoint Shane, no matter what." Although Stephanie hadn't received any of Jessica's calls, she knew her friend well enough that there is no way she would miss the kid's graduation.

Henry smiles at Carl and Jessica, nodding his head trying to soak in their truth. Just then, he hears a familiar voice,

"Is this seat taken?" Henry is so hoping it is Stephanie, but to his disappointment, it is Selma and Marcie Taylor.

"We can move down. I am watching out for Stephanie, but she hasn't arrived yet. Have a seat."

"Hello Selma, Marcie" says Carl. Marcie and Selma both say hello. Jessica says,

"We will be celebrating *you* Marcie next week, right?" Marcie trying to get comfortable in her seat yet beaming says,

"Yes, one more week." Jessica, sympathetic to Marcie's current pregnant state says,

"How you feeling?"

"Well Ms. Jessica, some days are better than others and this is one of the *other days*...but I wouldn't miss Jill's graduation...so here we are!" as she rubs her stomach.

The orchestra begins the march for the graduates. Henry looks around the gathering of people, but still no Stephanie.

§

A little out of breath Stephanie arrives in the arena just as the graduates were making their way to the stage. There were people everywhere. Stephanie found a seat in the upper level. She thinks,

"If my flight had been any later, I wouldn't have been able to live with myself. I should have followed my

first mind and come in last night." A woman
Stephanie sits next to says,

"It's alright sweetie catch your breath, they just
started walking in. You haven't missed a thing."
Stephanie letting out a deep sigh says,
"Thank you; I couldn't miss this for the world."

The woman just smiles as they watch the
commencement. Stephanie spots Shane as he walks
in, Stephanie sees him waves and assumes it is to
Henry but she still cannot spot him. As the graduates
continue to pour in, Stephanie notices Jill, and she
waves in the same general direction. Stephanie, still
scanning the crowd cannot locate Henry or the
Richardsons.

The audience gives a standing ovation as all two
hundred and sixty-five graduates take the stage. The
Dean takes his place at the podium and proceeds with
the program as written.

§

Henry appears to be as restless, while Madeleine Albright, former Secretary of State, delivers the graduation speech. Ms. Albright's charismatic demeanor and the sharing of her personal experiences are edifying and brings laughter to the crowd during most of her speech; Henry is still unengaged wondering about Stephanie.

"Did she make it, and if she didn't what would it do to Shane, and how would he explain." Henry's eyes begin to water; he knows that this present situation is entirely his fault. Carl, being the long time friend he is, placed his hand on Henry's shoulder and says,

"Man stop worrying. She is here, and she is here to stay." Henry nodding and sniffling says,

"Oh, you have a prophetic edge this morning." Carl laughs,

"Yes I do, and I know He is able." He gently places his palm on Jessica's hand to give Henry some hope of what could be for him and Stephanie.

§

For a private school, many families didn't observe the traditional holding of applause until all of the students receive their diplomas. Shane is next in line to receive his diploma as they call his name; he struts across the stage with super confidence. Stephanie holds to the four-year plan the Richardsons and McFinleys agree to. The agreement is when their children receive their diplomas; they will stand in admiration without applause. As she stands, she notices that Carl, Jessica and Henry also remember and stand. With tears falling down her face, Stephanie is so proud of Shane. Stephanie can see him recognize his Dad then Shane immediately looks around the arena; she knows he is looking for her. Stephanie sees Henry when he stands along with the Richardsons. She chuckles, "How could I miss those big guys" Just when she thought Shane doesn't see her, he kisses his diploma and blew the kiss to her. Stephanie crying harder returns the favor.

§

Henry, trying to hold his tears back nods in approval to Shane and his recent accomplishment. Henry and Carl high-five each other, Henry notices Shane scanning the row. He knows he is looking for Stephanie. Henry tries to be discreet and look around, but he doesn't see her. Just as he sits down, Henry notices Shane kissing his diploma and blowing a kiss. He knows Shane spots Stephanie, but he turns around and doesn't see her. Everything appears to be moving at such a fast pace. Just as Henry feels, he is comfortable in his seat; it is time to stand again. The dean calles, *"Jill Richardson."*

Jessica flies to her feet and let out a "Whew!" and one clap. Carl and Henry laugh, as Jill's eyes get big. She can't believe her mother did that. Jessica is covering her mouth and says,
"I got excited!"
"Rightfully so!" says Carl.

Henry immediately turns to see if he can see Stephanie, and to his surprise, he and Stephanie's eyes met. Henry raises his hand to say "hello". Stephanie did the same. Stephanie sits down and Henry is spell bound, until the man behind him says,

"Excuse me; can you have a seat, so we can see our son?" Henry snaps out of his *"Stephanie"* love stare and apologizes profusely to the couple behind him.

Henry's attention continues to be split between Shane's graduation and seeing his wife after the ceremony. Henry thinks,

"What will I say? What will she do?"

Interrupting Henry's thoughts is the valedictorian accepting the diplomas. The graduates and all the guests in the arena erupt in screams and applause for the graduating class. The graduates are hugging, high-fiving each other, male and females alike are shedding tears of joy. The school chaplain pronounces the blessing and the graduates exit the stage jumping and dancing.

There were so many people. Henry is glad they agreed on where to meet after the ceremony. As they walk out, Henry is looking for Stephanie and decides to call, but he is not getting a signal on his phone.

They reach their designated meeting place. Selma says, "That is a wonderful graduation, Madeleine

Albright is great. I have never heard her speak before." Jessica chimes in and says,

"Stephanie mentioned that she had the opportunity to hear her at a conference and spoke highly about how captivating she is." As Selma, Marcie and Jessica continue in small talk. Carl tries to calm his friend Henry.

"Hey man, can you believe it? They have graduated! All we have left is college, and we are home free!" Carl is trying to lighten the mood and calm Henry, but it obviously isn't working. Carl continues,

"Man, I haven't seen you this nervous since you were awaiting the announcement of your Heisman Trophy." Henry turns to Carl solemnly,

"Man, this moment is so much more important than that…I just want….I just…" Henry wipes his brow.

Carl says, "I know man, I know….you love her and you want her home. She is here Henry…here to stay. YOU do your part." Just as Henry is going to ask him what he means by that, Shane ran up behind him and jumps on his back.

"Hey Dad….I did it, and Stanford here I come!" Shane jumps down and hugs his dad. "Congratulations son!"

Jill immediately looks to the floor when she hears Shane say that. Jill and Shane have not spoken much since the whole college attendance blow up. The weight of Jill's thought disappears as her mom and dad bombarded her with their hugs and kisses.

"Sweetie, we are so proud of you," says Jessica. "Yeah, baby girl…Daddy is proud!" Jill saw Marcie and Ms. Selma."

Hey Marcie, thanks for coming!" Marcie and Jill hug and Shane receive his congratulations from Carl and

Jessica, as well as Selma and Marcie. Shane moves back toward his dad to ask,

"Where is Mom?" Just as he is asking, walking behind Henry he spots Stephanie. Shane dashes toward his mother with diploma in hand. He picks up his mother and starts kissing her saying, "Momma!" mocking Celie's son in the last scene of the *Color Purple.* Stephanie says,

"Shane Henry McFinley, if you don't put me down!" Everyone else just laughs. Even in this potentially tense moment, Shane stays true to his comedic bent and everyone is in laughter, mixed with tears, because of the reunion. Henry stands off intentionally as she greets everyone, so he can have her to himself and hoping she will not reject him.

Jessica, a little apprehensive, didn't have any idea how Stephanie would respond to her. But, fully believing in God's redemptive power and their years of friendship, Jessica holds out her arms and says,

"Diva!" Stephanie leans back and says "Diva!" Jessica and Stephanie embrace so long they couldn't help but turn to tears. Stephanie and Jessica rock back and forth as if their designer three-inch heels were a teeter-totter.

Jessica repeatedly asks Stephanie for forgiveness and tells her how much her friendship means to her. She thanks her for her help when she couldn't help herself. Stephanie repeatedly keeps telling Jessica, "I forgive you."

Selma passes out tissue for everyone, including Carl and Henry. Jill holds Shane's hand as her tears fall. Shane turns to Jill and wraps his arm around her. Jill leans into Shane and cries even harder. Shane rubs Jill's hair, kisses her on top of her forehead, and whispers.

"Jill, I do love you!" Jill holds her arms around Shane's waist and says,

"I love you too and don't want to be on separate coasts from you during school." Shane let out a sigh of relief and holds Jill as tight as he could.

After Jessica and Stephanie separate from their tearful reunion of forgiveness, Henry stands in the outer circle admiring his wife in her flowing white linen dress. He recognizes the butterfly printed cigar case purse he'd brought back from one of his business trips, but the natural colored, leather, three-inch sandals with leather straps that wraps around her ankles dangling with seashells, he has not seen. As always, her jewelry stood out, just as with each outfit. A chunky necklace of seashells and pearls intertwined flawlessly adorn her neck, along with a matching bracelet. She wears her hair pinned up in the back with the rest of her hair in perfect curls that surround her round face. Henry stares at Stephanie desperately wanting to hold her in his arms. As Stephanie pats the tears on her face, attempting not to disturb her makeup as much as possible, she mets Henry's face with her tear-filled eyes. Henry, in his standard custom Armani suit with cut away collar and fat knot tie, is handsome as ever; with his perfectly groomed beard, stands with arms open waiting for Stephanie.

Stephanie walks into Henry's arms. She nestles the top of her head just under his chin, closes her eyes and inhales all that she missed for the last two months. Henry's large arms embrace Stephanie's small frame and Stephanie, against everything in her, runs her small hands up Henry's back.

Henry soaking the moment in, breaks the silence and leans to Stephanie's ear and says,
"Baby, I miss you." He holds her and silently thanks God for another opportunity to hold his wife. Shane, as only Shane can do says,
"So a celebration is in order....let's eat!" Everyone laughs.

Stephanie, pulls back from Henry and looks at Shane, with confliction. Shane, knowing his mother is going to speak says,

"Mom, you are going to join us, right?"

"Of course son, but I have a five o'clock flight back to the beach house." The air appears to stand still around everyone. Carl looks to Henry to see how his old friend is reacting to the news. Jill squeezes Shane's hand to let him know she is there. Jessica, trying to change the awkward moment says,

"Oh come on, celebration is in order, reservations are waiting at La Châteaux d'Marco, right?" Jill smiles and tries to help things along also says,

"Yep, let's go...reservations wait." Stephanie shaking her head says, "Yep let's go. I will meet you all there." Stephanie turns on her heals and walked away.

Shane, with tears in his eyes, looks at Henry and says, "Dad?" Henry, paralyzed, watches the tears fall down Shane's face. Carl moves toward Henry and says, "You know what you need to do!"

Henry grabsShane in the back of his head holds him in his arms and says, "Son, go with Uncle Carl and Aunt Jessica...I am going to make it right."

Henry, without further delay turns and Stephanie is nowhere in sight. He thinks, *"Where could she have gone?"* Henry briskly walks around the arena to the next set of doors. There were so many people. He almost panics and thinks,

"I can't loose her... not again!"

He hopes that as he turns the corner he will see Stephanie. He does not spot her. Henry's brisk walk is turning into a mild dash that is picking up speed as if he is running down the football field. Weaving and towering over guests, trying to take pictures and exiting the arena, Henry is trying to locate Stephanie in the crowd. He is looking out the windows as he is running to the exit to see if he can see her. Henry's gigantic structure overlooks most of the guests. Running and shouting

"Excuse me….Sorry…Coming through… Excuse me, Sorry, Sorry."

Henry takes the next door out of the arena. He stands on the steps hoping the height of the steps, along with his natural height, will give him an advantage to locate Stephanie in the crowd. He would normally look for her bouncing hair as she struts with her runway walk, but he recalls her hair is not down but in an up-do. Just as he scans the crowd for the third time, Henry locates Stephanie. He calls out to her

"Stephanie…Stephanie…Stephanie…" Henry starts moving through the crowd keeping his eyes on her. Henry continues to call out,

"Stephanie….Stephanie…Stephanie…" there are hundreds of people, how is she going to hear him? Henry recalls Pastor Matthew's words, *"You have to fight."* Henry, determined and with a fight, calls out again much louder and says,

"Stephanie….Stephanie…Stephanie…" Henry starts to belt in his rich tenor voice one of the songs Stephanie marked on Brian McKnight's *Evolution of a Man* CD[i]; and he sang

"If I traveled all around the world
I know what I would find
Someone half as smart
Someone half as sweet
Half as lovely and half as kind;
If I is the ruler of
A kingdom with a house of wives to choose
It wouldn't even quite compare
To what I've got right here with you…"

The groups of people around the arena start to get quiet as they listen to Henry serenade Stephanie from afar. Whispers and looks of bewilderment serve as a background to Henry's singing. Stephanie hearing Henry's voice stops in her tracks. Without turning around, she recognizes that melodious voice anywhere. Henry continues to move toward Stephanie singing.

"...So if I stumble just a bit
trying to say what's on my mind
Please excuse me cuz I never felt
the way that I feel inside
It's possible
I may have finally have found my dream come true
There can never be another you..."

As Henry walks closer to Stephanie, the crowd moves out of his way parting a path as if it is a staged scene of a romantic Life Time movie. When Henry reaches Stephanie, he places his hands on her shoulders, turns her toward him, and sings directly to her, not moving his eyes from hers. Stephanie's face covered in tears submits to Henry's positioning. Stephanie is so overwhelmed. She has not heard Henry sing to her since their wedding and he is now singing in front of hundreds of people a song she selected for their vow renewal. Henry wipes her tears with his handkerchief and continues to sing;

"...The stars are bright tonight
they know you are mine all mine
I knew that it would be alright when my other dreams
fell through
and for this very night I've waited all my life
standing straight and tall
I give my all to you..."

With every heartfelt emotion in Henry and his
melodious, skillful run of the musical scale, Henry
continues his public display of affection by further
surprising Stephanie by inserting his own words to her

"...So please excuse me if I
Stumbled just a bit
Trying to say what's on my mind
Please excuse me cuz I know that I have felt the way
that I feel inside
and yes it's possible, I know Stephanie you are my
dream come true

There can never be another you
There can never be another you"

With rousing applause and screams from the crowd.
Stephanie fell into Henry's arms. Henry refusing to
hold back his tears loves on Stephanie and says,

"Don't leave Stephanie. The last sixty days have been
hell on earth for me. I do not want to know what life is
without you. You are everything to me; the air I
breathe the reason why I sing. You are all I ever
wanted and I knew that from the start. You are good
for me. You opened my heart…something no one else
could do…do not leave. I recommit to showing you
everything you mean to me. There will be no question
in your mind regarding my intentions toward you and
our family."

Henry moves his hands from Stephanie's shoulders
and gently places her head between his hands wiping
her tears with his thumbs.

"…There is so much I want to say… Babe, God has forgiven me, but I need you to forgive me." Stephanie still crying is taking everything in from Henry. A long piercing silence is broken when Stephanie says,

"Henry, my heart is so wounded. You have to know that I have never stopped wanting you and my love for you has fueled that wanting …but I know that God can mend my heart, if I allow him to, and that's the truth. …" Henry smiled and with Stephanie in his arms, he passionately kisses her. Stephanie, with completely no fight in her welcomes the quiver up her back and graciously receives her husband's kiss. When Henry finally releases Stephanie's lips he says,

"Mrs. Stephanie McFinley….that is the healing truth."

Order the pre-sequels of the *"Covenant of Lies"* series at www.monarchpublicationsllc.webs.com, www.amazon.com or other major book resellers.

See what others are saying about
"Covenant of Lies The Revealed Truth".
Second in the series

COVENANT OF LIES THE REVEALED TRUTH (the 2nd book in the series) is a fast-paced novel that continues the story of the Richardson, McFinley and Taylor families (along with a few others). Get ready for a roller coaster ride to expose and "reveal" the personal and spiritual journey in faith and forgiveness that each character has to bear. This book is sure to please and tease the reading fans of author Holly Spence long after the last page is turns.

Personal Note:
You are a welcome addition to the Christian fiction genre. Looking forward to the "healing" finale!

A.M. Boclair, Founder
B.R.A.N.C.H.E.S.
Boclair's Reading Association – Nurturing Change, Healing, Empowerment & Sitsisfaction

Purchase the Covenant series,
"Covenant of Lies The Revealed Truth"

See additional books by author Holly Spence

HOLLY SPENCE

See what others are saying about this dynamic

publication;

"The heart issues that you describe are right on...All servants, even those who are leaders can benefit from preparing a heart to serve."

Dr. Rodney Swope
Rod & Staff Enterprises
www.rodnstaff.net

"We often need a goad to cause us to stop and take the time to reaffirm our commitment to Christ and service others as an outflow of that commitment. This book offers good biblical and comical anecdotes to cause us to pause in our journey reflect and readjust our hearts."

Elder Monica Keenon
iSucseed, LLC
isucseed@hotmail.com

"WARNING: WHAT YOU ARE ABOUT TO READ MAY BE DANGEROUS TO YOUR SPIRTUAL AND POLITICAL HEALTH!"

"Servant Leadership The Heart That Serves" **is also available on a 2-CD audio disc.**

 **Disc 1**   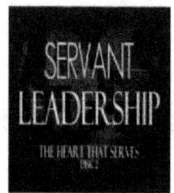 **Disc 2**

Servant Leadership is available for corporate bible studies and may be purchased in bulk please contact Monarch Publications, LLC at monarchpublicationsllc@yahoo.com

You've rendered an excellent program of empowerment. Very nicely done! Good flow. Nice overlaps between key topics. I especially liked the areas where you completely turn loose and throw the fire of your personality into it. That fire is "you" and makes the book. Very impressive methodology. Keep it up!

Larry Trujillo
Principal Consultant
Oracle Corporation

I think your book so far is well laid out, easy to read, interactive and engaging. Each chapter I've read, entices me to participate in the process and the activities. It's very applicable to life, not just work.

Cindy Dutra
Oracle Corporation

Well I have a 2-year-old son and a 3.5-year-old daughter and even though they are not in school, I still run around like a chicken with my head cut off. Sometimes you have to take 10 minutes to just calm down, but sometimes Holly it's not possible. I always worked a 9 to 5 or 9 to 8 before I had kids. I'm trying to get this online business situated plus my own business situated so I will have more than 10 minutes to relax. I've seen it done and I see it being done. You know what my 10 minutes consist of? Giving back whether it be advice, whether it just be thanking God for all he has done for me and people who've I've come in contact with. Even though I don't lay my head to rest until 11 sometimes 12, I still feel my mind working. But you have given me something to think about. RELAX, RELATE, RELEASE!

Annie McCall

Workshops are currently being scheduled for corporate entry-level management, senior executives, church leadership and team workshops.

For workshop information and speaking engagement requests please send an email to <u>monarchpublcaitonsllc@yahoo.com</u>

Appendix

---

[i] Another You by Brian McKnight Evolution of a Man